Time Warped

> Five Read-Aloud Plays that
> S-t-r-e-t-c-h the Truth
> about the Past
>
> The Mummy's Purse
> The Idiodyssey
> The Schmikings
> There's No Ages Like Dark Ages
> Renaissance Reform School

Bruce Berger

illustrated by Larry Nolte

Cottonwood Press, Inc.
Fort Collins, Colorado

Copyright © 2001 by Cottonwood Press, Inc. All rights reserved.

Permission is granted to reproduce the plays and activities in this book, in other than electronic form, for the purchaser's own personal use in the classroom, provided that the copyright notice appears on each reproduction. Otherwise, no part of this work may be reproduced or transmitted in any form or by any means without written permission from Cottonwood Press, Inc.

Requests for permission should be addressed to:

Cottonwood Press, Inc.
107 Cameron Drive
Fort Collins, Colorado 80525
800-864-4297
e-mail: cottonwood@cottonwoodpress.com

www. cottonwoodpress.com

ISBN 1-877673-46-3

Printed in the United States of America

To my son Adam and daughter, TESS,
Pat Weiss,
all the wonderful and supportive
colleagues and students of Barrington School District #220,
but, most importantly, to the man who gave me
guidance, courage, love, and endless encouragement:
my father,
William A. Berger, Sr.

Table of Contents

The Mummy's Purse 11
The Idiodyssey 33
The Schmikings 55
There's No Ages Like Dark Ages 75
Renaissance Reform School 95

INTRODUCTION

Ah, radio plays! They truly are a forgotten frontier of educational and entertainment exploration. I wrote the plays in *Time Warped* for students to use in the classroom as mock radio programs, complete with sound effects. However, the plays have been adapted so that they can also be used as read-aloud plays, or even as plays to perform. Feel free to use them any way you wish.

Radio plays. To get started, have a discussion with your group to discover what your students know about radio plays. Ask them if they have ever heard any recordings of old radio programs from the 1920s through the 1950s. If they haven't, there are many recordings of old radio programs available at libraries, book stores and music centers. The "skits" written by Garrison Keillor from the current radio program *Prairie Home Companion* are widely available. Play some of these recordings for the class to give your students a frame of reference before they read these plays.

To produce the plays in your classroom, divide the class into groups of about eight to twelve students each, depending on the length of the play you assign to each group. The groups should have a mixture of boys and girls, as well as a mixture of reading abilities. Heterogeneous grouping encourages students to help each other as they analyze the plot of a play, determine the meanings and pronunciations of new vocabulary words, interpret the lines and select appropriate sound effects.

Give a copy of the play to each member of the group and allow the students themselves to assign the roles for each play. Rearrange the classroom for round table reading so students are able to hear and see one another. Either arrange the desks in groups or move them to the side of the room to provide floor space.

As the teacher, your role should be that of facilitator, rather than director. Circulate from group to group and help with any trouble spots. Since these were originally written as radio plays, sound effects are indicated throughout each play. Remind each group that they need to decide how to produce the sound effects indicated in the script, and encourage them to brainstorm additional sound effects that would improve the production of the play. (Experimenting with sounds also adds a certain amount of the enjoyment to the practice sessions.) The amount of time you spend practicing in class is up to you, but before the plays are recorded, have a dress rehearsal for each group.

For the final recording of a group's production, place a good tape recorder in the front of the room. Have the rest of the class act as the studio audience. You can even invite parents to attend the production. The characters gather around the microphone, reading their

Introduction

lines in turn. As the recording engineer, you should be ready to press "pause" whenever difficulties arise. The advantage to recording the play is that you can rewind the tape and redo the mistakes.

These recordings can be enjoyed throughout the year. You can place copies of exceptional performances by individual students in their portfolios. Students can also check out the tapes to take home.

Read aloud plays. If you decide to use the plays as read-aloud plays, rather than radio plays, simply assign a student (or several students) to play the "role" of "Sound Effects." As the play is read aloud, these students hum or sing whenever music is noted in the script. They simulate other sound effects, as noted, using their ingenuity and whatever resources they can find in the room.

After students read aloud one play, don't be surprised if the "Sound Effects" roles become the most sought-after roles in subsequent plays.

Live performances. With just a bit of adapting, the plays can also be performed as skits. Simply have the narrators sit on stools at either side of the stage or performing area. Sound effects can be recorded and played off stage, or performed "live" off stage. A bit of creativity can go a long way!

As students read the plays, they will encounter historical "facts" that apparently contradict existing records. They can research the suggested topics given at the end of each play to explore what experts consider the real story. Further activities in the book provide many opportunities to integrate subject matter from elsewhere in the curriculum. Some students may even choose to try their hand at writing some "historically fractured" radio plays of their own.

Whatever you do, don't forget that these plays aren't to be taken too seriously. Allow your students, and yourself, to have a good time!

Bruce Berger

THE MUMMY'S PURSE

The Mummy's Purse

CHARACTERS

Narrator #1

Narrator #2

Charles Cartomb (car-TOMB). A very dignified Egyptian government leader.

Dr. Benjamin Butterball. A distinguished archaeologist, specializing in Egyptology.

Dr. Mary Leafy. A young archaeologist who works with Dr. Butterball and who doesn't take things nearly as seriously as he does.

Pharaoh Fufu (FOO-foo). A female Egyptian mummy who comes to life.

Emperor Zero. An emperor of ancient Rome.

Tribune Nausius (NAW-ze-us). Emperor Zero's aide.

Superficia. (soo-pur-FISH-ee-uh). Emperor Zero's shallow wife.

Numerius (new-MARE-ee-us). Emperor Zero's soothsayer.

Spirit #1

Spirit #2

Spirit #3

Spirit #4

Hammable (HAM-muh-bul). A military general from Carthage.

Armanius (are-MON-ee-us). A clothing designer from Carthage.

Smucker. An advisor in Pharaoh Fufu's court.

Voice #1

Voice #2

Voice #3

Julius Sneezer. A young general from Rome.

Sound Effects. This "role" can be performed by a group of people. If the play is recorded as a radio show or performed in front of a group, the sound effects can be prepared carefully ahead of time. If the play is read aloud in class, quick and easy methods of simulating sound effects should be improvised as the play is read. For example, the sound effects group might hum when music is specified, or drop books on a desk top when crashing noises are indicated.

Setting: The present day. An archaeological site in Egypt.

Narrator #1: The mysteries of Ancient Egypt have long attracted the interest of learned men and women all over the world. The Sphinx and the pyramids hold a special fascination for scientists like Dr. Benjamin Butterball and Dr. Mary Leafy.

The Mummy's Purse

Narrator #2: Let's listen in as these well-known archaeologists visit an Egyptian tomb . . .

Cartomb: Dr. Butterball, Dr. Leafy — Welcome! It is indeed a pleasure that my government has allowed me to join you today.

Butterball: Thank you, Mr. Cartomb. After all our years of research at the United States Polytechnical Institute for the Archaeologically Challenged, we are truly overjoyed at the prospects of a unique discovery. Isn't that correct, Dr. Leafy?

Leafy: (*Sighing*) Right. I'm tickled pink to be here in the Land of the Pharaohs . . . Is it always this hot in these pyramids?

Cartomb: Actually, it hasn't been this cool in a week. Whatever I can do to aid in your research, consider me at your service.

Butterball: What's this? Here, Dr. Leafy! Look! This must be the secret passageway to the burial chamber of Pharaoh Ramamoose *(RAM-uh-moose)*.

Leafy: Oh, no, not again. For the past four weeks it's always the same thing: "This must be the secret passageway to the burial chamber of Pharaoh Ramamoose." It's probably just another laundry chute.

Cartomb: No, Dr. Leafy. Dr. Butterball is correct. I have been in this pyramid hundreds of times and have never before seen this passage.

Sound Effects: *Sound of small rocks falling.*

Cartomb: (*Continuing*) Be careful, Doctor, that wall is moving!

Sound Effects: *Sound of large stones sliding, followed by a crashing sound.*

Cartomb: Dr. Butterball, are you all right?

Butterball: (*From a distance*) Yes, yes, I've fallen, but I *can* get up. I am fine. Hand down a flashlight.

Sound Effects: *Clicking sound of flashlight turning on and off.*

Butterball: I don't see much down here. Wait! What's this? . . . Why this is very peculiar! It's a curious satchel of some sort. There are some strange hieroglyphics written on the outside. Here. Help me up.

Leafy: Can you translate them, Doctor? Here's your manual: *Mummies for Dummies.*

Butterball: I believe so. (*Reading*) "The Curse of the Purse awaits all who disturb the contents of the wallet within."

Leafy: Sounds inviting! There must be some credit cards in there.

Butterball: I'm looking . . . This did not belong to Ramamoose.

Leafy: How can you tell?

BUTTERBALL: Here's a card that says: "If lost or stolen, return to Pharaoh Fufu."

LEAFY: Pharaoh Fufu? Who's he?

BUTTERBALL: Not "he." Pharaoh Fufu is a "she." Look at the photo I.D.

LEAFY: A female pharaoh? Like the famous Hatshepsut *(hat-SHEP-soot)*, who ruled in the 15th century B.C.?

BUTTERBALL: Quite right, Dr. Leafy. But unlike Hatshepsut, there is no record anywhere of this Pharaoh Fufu.

LEAFY: Are you certain?

BUTTERBALL: In my 52 years of studying ancient Egypt, I have never encountered anything at all about a Pharaoh Fufu.

CARTOMB: I can echo that claim, Doctor.

BUTTERBALL: I wonder what's inside this . . .

LEAFY: Doctor, wait! Remember the warning? The curse on the purse?

BUTTERBALL: Nonsense. I am a scientist, not a purse snatcher. I am endeavoring to unlock a doorway to the past. Dr. Leafy, the key lies within this purse. I'm not worried. What could possibly happen?

SOUND EFFECTS: *Thunderous rumbling, followed by sinister music.*

LEAFY: Oh, I don't know; maybe a wall could slide open, a brilliant light could blind our senses, and a mysterious figure could appear in the dust.

FUFU: *(In a booming voice)* Who dares to violate the contents of the purse?

CARTOMB: Please spare us. We are not robbers.

BUTTERBALL: Yes! We are mere scientists.

LEAFY: Actually, I'm not even with them. Listen, is there a ladies' restroom around here?

BUTTERBALL: *(Sarcastically, to Dr. Leafy)* Thank you, Miss Loyalty!

FUFU: Silence! A dismal death awaits all who disturb the treasures of the purse of —

SOUND EFFECTS: *Crashing sound as she falls.*

FUFU: *(Continuing)* Owww! Oh, I hate these wrappings. And now I've broken a nail!

LEAFY: Are you all right? Here let me help you up.

BUTTERBALL: Are you the guardian of the purse?

FUFU: Guardian? Hey, that *is* my purse!

LEAFY: You mean, *you* are Pharaoh Fufu?

FUFU: Pharaoh Fufunahton *(Foo-fun-AH-tun)* to the peasants, if you please.

CARTOMB: Our humblest apologies, your highness. A thousand pardons . . .

FUFU: Knock off the baloney. I'll spare your feeble lives if you help get these wrappings off me.

BUTTERBALL: Thank you, thank you, thank you! You must understand — It's just that we've never heard of you before and . . .

FUFU: What? Never heard of me? Why, I was the greatest pharaoh in the history of Egypt!

BUTTERBALL: In all the research that has ever been done, and there has been a lot of it, scientists have found very little evidence of female pharaohs. Pharaohs were almost always men.

LEAFY: And what's more, there never was one with a ridiculous name like Pharaoh Fufu.

FUFU: Hey, watch it, sister. People in glass pyramids shouldn't throw stones. With a name like "Leafy," you're in no position to criticize.

BUTTERBALL: Dr. Leafy, don't anger the (*Spelling*) M-U-M-M-Y.

FUFU: Hey, we're all adults here. Don't spell things. Just spit out what you want to say. Who are the rest of you, and what are you doing in my neck of the woods?

BUTTERBALL: I am Dr. Benjamin Butterball. This is my research assistant, Dr. Mary Leafy. This is Charles Cartomb of the Egyptian government. We are seeking the keys to unlocking the past of ancient Egypt. Can you tell us — Were all the pharaohs really women?

FUFU: Sure, at least all the ones before me. Let's see. There was Pharaoh Felicia, my great, great-grandmother . . . Pharaoh Phoebe, my great-grandmother . . . Pharaoh Fanny, my . . .

LEAFY: Let me guess: your grandmother?

FUFU: Why, yes! How did you know?

LEAFY: Lucky guess.

FUFU: And then there was Pharaoh Faucett, my mother.

BUTTERBALL: Pharaoh Faucett?

FUFU: Oh, yes. She installed indoor plumbing in all the pyramids.

CARTOMB: Wait! Why would you need plumbing? The pyramids were tombs for the pharaohs when they passed to the afterlife.

FUFU: Oh, no. The pyramids were all hotels.

BUTTERBALL: Hotels?

FUFU: Of course. People came from miles around to stay in them and shop at the Gaza Strip Mall. *(Proudly)* During my reign I was known as "The Shopping Queen of the Nile."

CARTOMB: This is unbelievable! Why have I never read of this before?

FUFU: It must have been our scribes. Good help was hard to find during my mother's rule, so they began allowing men to record the events of our day. And you know what lousy secretaries men are. They must have just rewritten the entire text of the history.

LEAFY: Well, it wouldn't be the first time.

BUTTERBALL: Ladies! Aren't you being just a wee bit sexist in your thinking here? Also, I have a hard time believing all this. Majestic One, perhaps you could provide us with more details to your story.

FUFU: All right. Where should I begin? Let's see . . . Egypt has always been the "Cradle of Civilization," but it really wasn't until I became pharaoh that trade began to flourish and Egypt became the commercial capital of the world. Of course, that was following the Tunic Wars.

CARTOMB: Tunic Wars?

FUFU: Yes, the Tunic Wars between Carthage and Rome.

BUTTERBALL: Don't you mean *Punic* Wars? You know, the wars between Carthage and Rome, starting in 246 B.C., for the control of North Africa?

FUFU: No, no, it was the *Tunic* Wars. You see, Rome and Carthage were the two top manufacturers of military menswear. They were constantly trying to steal each other's designs. If it hadn't been for me and my purse, there would never have been any economic stability in the ancient world. You see, it all began in Rome with Emperor Zero.

NARRATOR #1: As Pharaoh Fufu tells her version of history, we go back in time, to ancient Rome. The famous Emperor Zero, who later played the cello while his country burned, is in his office.

NARRATOR #2: Emperor Zero is very worried. He is pacing back and forth when his aide, Tribune Nausius, enters.

GOING BACK IN TIME . . .

NAUSIUS: Emperor Zero! Emperor Zero!

ZERO: Yes, Tribune Nausius. What is it?

NAUSIUS: Emperor, the plebeians (plu-BE-uns) are revolting!

Zero: Tell me about it! At the last banquet, they got more food on their clothes than they got in their mouths.

Nausius: No, not "revolting" that way. They are getting ready to begin a revolution to overthrow your government.

Zero: Blast those plebeians! All they ever do is whine and complain.

Nausius: Well, Emperor, there have been several layoffs at the clothing stores and state sweatshops. The unemployment level has reached 13½ percent. What is more, Senator Malicious has been holding secret meetings at the Forum. Emperor Zero, I believe he is plotting against you.

Zero: Senator Malicious? He's never liked me. Nobody likes me! I'm so depressed. Hand me my cello — and that turkey leg over there, too. *(Seeing his wife enter)* Hello, Superficia *(Soo-pur-FISH-ee-uh)*, my little cupcake.

Superficia: Zero, I have nothing to wear to the banquet tonight.

Zero: Superficia, you have six closets full of togas and tunics.

Superficia: I have nothing *decent* to wear, and I can't even buy anything. All the clothing stores keep saying there is nothing in stock. Everything is on backorder. I wanted to get something from that new designer, Calvin Kleinius.

Nausius: But we haven't produced even one of his garments, and it's been over four months now. If you aren't careful, Emperor, he will move to Carthage, just like Armanius did.

Zero: Well, do something!

Nausius: We just need to get the raw materials, Emperor Zero. The fields in the south of Gaul could supply us with more cotton than we could ever use.

Superficia: Well, tell him to go get it, Zero. You're the emperor, aren't you?

Zero: It is not that easy, sugar plum. Gaul won't extend us any further credit, and the treasury of Rome is limited after all the military conquests.

Superficia: Well, take it by force, you spineless jellyfish! You're the leader of Rome. Everybody is petrified of Rome.

Nausius: It is not that easy, Empress. The Gauls may burn their fields in protest if we take the country by force.

Superficia: Oh, hush, Nausius! Don't be so negative. You make me sick!

Zero: He's right, buttercup. If Gaul fears an attack, the cotton fields could go up in smoke.

Superficia: Oh, those Gauls. They've got a lot of gall! Listen, Zero, you had better solve this problem or I will make your life miserable. And you know I can do it, too. I'll see you at the banquet. *(She exits)*

ZERO: *(With a heavy sigh)* By the beard of Apollo, whatever am I going to do? No raw materials, no treasury to get the raw materials, and an acid-tongued wife who will soon make my life even more miserable, if I'm not careful. Oh, woe is me!

NAUSIUS: Wait! I have an idea! Perhaps we could ask Soothsayer Numerius for a solution to this problem.

ZERO: Of course! With his second sight, Soothsayer Numerius could guide us to the source of the gold we need to buy the raw materials. Then I won't be sleeping on the hideaway lounge in the guest palace. Send for Numerius!

NAUSIUS: *(Calling)* Send for Numerius!

VOICE 1: *(From a distance)* Send for Numerius!

VOICE 2: *(From further away)* Send for Numerius!

VOICE 3: *(From still further away)* Send for Numerius!

NAUSIUS: He must be down in the catacombs again.

ZERO: Well, while we wait, I must say that this plan is nothing short of brilliant on your part, Nausius. If we are successful, you shall receive a promotion in rank.

NAUSIUS: Oh, thank you, Emperor Zero! Ah — here is Numerius now.

ZERO: Ah, Numerius. Come in, come in. We need your second sight here.

NUMERIUS: *(Chanting)* Aha, maha, daha. Eware-bay the ookies-cay of Arch-way!

NAUSIUS: Knock off the pig Latin, Numerius. We're in a real pickle here.

NUMERIUS: So, Emperor, what can I do for you?

ZERO: Numerius, you have served Rome well in the past, and I hope you can deliver the bacon once again.

NUMERIUS: Ooh . . . yum. Does this have something to do with fast-food restaurants? A cheeseburger with bacon . . . a chicken filet with bacon . . .

ZERO: No, no, Numerius. Attend to what I say. Our clothing manufacturing monopoly on the civilized world is in serious jeopardy. Unemployment in the state sweatshops is soaring. Calvin Kleinius is getting ready to skip town for Carthage. My wife is barking for a new clothing line. Worst of all, the raw material cupboards are as bare as the Roman Treasury Department!

NUMERIUS: All rightie. So where do I come in, Emp?

ZERO: We want you to use your second sight to find some pushover's land that is loaded with gold — so we can loot it! Then we'll buy the raw materials we need and produce a blue-light special line of tunics that will bring Carthage to its manufacturing knees.

The Mummy's Purse

NUMERIUS: I get the picture now. I'll do my best. Let me tune into my second sight here . . .

(*Chanting*)

Uhmm! Uhmm! Oyais-oyais-oyais!

Meeska mooska crocodile.
Hear me, spirits of the Nile.

Give me the info Zero needs,
or he won't have a prayer to succeed.

Oh-Wa-Ta-Goo-Siam.
Phony Baloney, Calizony.

The spirits are about to speak!

SOUND EFFECTS: *Cymbals crash as Numerius goes into a trance. Spirit voices are heard coming from his body.*

SPIRIT #1: (*Chanting*)

The gold, they tell us, from Hammurabi's palace
reached halfway to the moon.

SPIRIT #2: (*Chanting*)

The blinding blur of the treasure of Ur
was a wonder to make you swoon.

SPIRIT #3: (*Chanting*)

But these treasures so rare can never compare
with the wealth of an Egyptian queen.

SPIRIT #4: (*Chanting*)

With Pharaoh Fufu's purse you could do no worse
in conquering the clothing scene!

ZERO: Is that all?

SPIRITS #1-4: (*Together, chanting or singing to the tune of "There's No Business Like Show Business"*)

There's no business, like clothes business,
like no business, I know.

ZERO: Okay, Numerius, we get the point.

Spirits #1-4:

Everything about it *seams* appealing.
Everything the seamstress will allow.

Zero: Nausius, will you pull the plug on them already? Better yet, throw a bucket of water on Numerius.

Sound Effects: *Sound of a big splash.*

Spirits #1-4: *(Spoken slowly and gradually getting softer and softer)*

Oh, what a world, what a wicked Roman world!
We're melting; we're melting!

Numerius: *(Coming out of his trance)* Hey, what's the big idea! I'm soaking wet. Who threw the water on me?

Zero: Noble Numerius, it was the only way to rescue you from the grip of your trance.

Nausius: You were really full of the spirits today! They were wailing something fierce.

Numerius: That happens sometimes. Did you get all the information you desired, Emp?

Zero: Yes, thank you, Numerius. Pharaoh Fufu has the gold we need! Nausius, give Numerius an extra denarius for his efforts.

Numerius: *(Trying to shake himself dry)* I'd settle for a beach towel.

Zero: We must make haste, boys. If this Pharaoh Fufu's got the gold, an army has to —

Nausius: Emperor Zero, taking Egypt by force may not be the answer.

Zero: You don't think so?

Nausius: No. If she has a hefty purse, she could raise an army of considerable strength. Fighting back would tax our already taxed treasury.

Zero: Well, what do you propose, Tribune Nausius?

Nausius: Let's send a well-spoken representative who can strike a steadfast alliance with this wealthy queen. Let's get her on our side and lure her into sponsoring Calvin Kleinius's new clothing line.

Zero: Hmmm! What do you think, Numerius?

Numerius: It sounds like pretty sound logic to me.

Zero: Then let it be done. What well-spoken representative can we send? Who do we have on call at the moment here in Rome?

Nausius: Well, there's Consul Flabbius.

ZERO: No, he eats too much.

NAUSIUS: Consul Gabbius?

ZERO: No, he talks too much. Wait a minute. Who's that young general who kept falling off his horse all the time in Gaul?

NAUSIUS: (*Laughing*) Oh, you mean Julius Sneezer?

ZERO: That's the guy.

NAUSIUS: (*Incredulous*) You want to send *him*? He's a klutz! And he always starts sneezing when he gets nervous.

ZERO: I know, but he's good-looking. We need to send someone who'll be attractive to the queen of the Nile. We need someone who can sweet talk her into backing us. Numerius, what does your second sight think of Julius Sneezer?

NUMERIUS: Looks good to me.

ZERO: Great! Then send for Julius Sneezer!

VOICE 1: (*Calling*) Send for Sneezer!

VOICE 2: (*From further away*) Send for Sneezer!

VOICE 3: (*From still further away*) Send for Sneezer!

> **SOUND EFFECTS:** *Sneezes are heard in the distance, slowly getting louder and louder as Julius Sneezer approaches.*

SNEEZER: (*Entering*) Achoo! Did you send for me, Emperor Zero?

ZERO: Yes. I want you to get us all the money we need to put Calvin Kleinius's designs into production.

SNEEZER: (*Most violent sneeze yet*) Achoo!!! Say what? How am I supposed to find that kind of money?

ZERO: Julius, my boy, have you ever been to Egypt?

COMING BACK TO THE PRESENT . . .

NARRATOR #1: Suddenly, back in modern day Egypt, Dr. Butterball cannot bear to listen to any more of Pharaoh Fufu's version of history.

NARRATOR #2: Frustrated, he interrupts the mummy's story.

BUTTERBALL: Pharaoh Fufu, hold on here a moment. All of what you are saying totally contradicts everything recorded in ancient history.

CARTOMB: Quite right, your highness. Just as an example, there was never a man named Julius Sneezer. He was Julius *Caesar*.

FUFU: Hey, were you there, Charlie?

CARTOMB: Well, um, no.

FUFU: Then put a sock in it.

LEAFY: So did this Julius Sneezer actually come to see you? Did you give him the money that Rome needed to produce the clothes?

FUFU: Hold your horses, honey. I'll get to that, but first you have to hear about Carthage and General Hammable.

BUTTERBALL: Er, uh, Pharaoh, don't you mean *Hannibal?*

FUFU: Who's telling this story, Butterball, me or you?

BUTTERBALL: Sorry, please go on. I'll keep silent.

FUFU: Good! While Zero and Rome struggled with their problems, General Hammable and his city of Carthage were having clothes production problems of their own. General Hammable was very angry with his designer, Armanius . . .

GOING BACK IN TIME . . .

HAMMABLE: Armanius, your line of military wear stinks!!!

ARMANIUS: General Hammable, what do you mean by that? Everyone I have spoken with just loves my designs.

HAMMABLE: Plaid! Who wears plaid into battle, unless they're Scottish? And what's more, my officers have informed me that the tunics you have designed catch fire with the first flaming arrow shot. My soldiers are flaring up like Roman candles! Do you know what our enemies are calling me?

ARMANIUS: No, sir.

HAMMABLE: They're calling me Flammable Hammable! This will not look good in history books!

ARMANIUS: A thousand pardons, general. I shall start working on a new design right away.

HAMMABLE: How can we ever corner the world market on military wear when we manufacture products like these? No one will buy from us. Rome will soon control the entire market.

ARMANIUS: I swear I shall have a new design by the first of the month.

HAMMABLE: Good. Now get out! Get out! *(Armanius exits.)* How am I supposed to control my blood pressure with situations like this! Worse, my physicians say they are running out of leeches. If it's not one thing, it's another . . .*(Armanius enters again.)* What? Armanius? You're back already? What is it this time?

The Mummy's Purse

ARMANIUS: Sir, I have just received word from my sources in Rome that Julius Sneezer is traveling to Egypt to seek Pharaoh Fufu's purse! Rome cannot afford to produce its next line of tunics. Emperor Zero hopes that Sneezer will be able to charm Fufu into giving Rome money.

HAMMABLE: Sneezer? Ah . . . Perhaps this is our chance to put Rome out of business. Zero must be stopped! Rome must *not* get the money to back his line of tunics. I shall go and seek the purse myself. I will beat Zero at his own game.

ARMANIUS: Beware of Pharaoh Fufu, general. I have heard that she cannot be trusted.

HAMMABLE: Well, neither can I. Armanius, go and fetch us the swiftest horses. We shall leave immediately.

NARRATOR #1: The first to arrive in Egypt was Sneezer.

NARRATOR #2: He did not succeed in charming Pharaoh Fufu out of the sacred purse. He did, however, benefit from her boxes of Kleenex.

NARRATOR #1: After Sneezer had drained Egypt of its supply of Kleenex, Hammable showed up. Pharaoh Fufu's page announced his arrival . . .

SMUCKER: Announcing General Flammable, the high leader of Carthage!

HAMMABLE: That's Hammable! Not flammable!

SMUCKER: Announcing General Hammable, the high leader of Carthage!

HAMMABLE: Greetings to you, noble Queen of the Nile. I hope you have not promised the gold from your purse to Sneezer to sponsor those rotten Roman rags.

FUFU: No. The only thing we have guaranteed him is this king size beach towel for blowing his nose.

HAMMABLE: Noble Queen, I must tell you that the rightful manufacturing ruler of the clothing world should be Carthage, not Rome. Our new line of tunics from the dapper designer Armanius will have all of Europe and Asia dressed in the highest of fashion elegance.

SNEEZER: (*Sneezing*) Don't listen to him, Queen Fufu. You've seen our designs. Calvin Kleinius's artistic apparel is far more worthy of your backing than those cheesy Carthage capes.

FUFU: Be silent! Both of you! I shall consult with my oldest and wisest advisor here. Smucker, gather the designs from both of them, and we shall study them in peace and quiet.

HAMMABLE: He's your oldest advisor? He looks so young.

FUFU: Well, Smucker is well preserved.

SNEEZER: Is there anything I can do for you, Queen, to influence your decision? I am at your disposal.

FUFU: First take out the garbage.

SNEEZER: Very well, your highness.

FUFU: Then peel me another grape. And try not to sneeze on it this time.

SNEEZER: Right away.

HAMMABLE: I can peel it better than he can, Pharaoh Fufu. Give me that grape!

SOUND EFFECTS: *Sound of a scuffle.*

SNEEZER: No, she asked me to do it first . . .

FUFU: Let us go, Smucker. We will study the designs in peace and quiet and let these two fight it out. (*Fufu and Smucker exit.*)

HAMMABLE: Sneezer, wait! Look over there.

SNEEZER: What is it? More grapes?

HAMMABLE: Isn't that Pharaoh Fufu's purse?

SNEEZER: I think you're right. What's inside?

SOUND EFFECTS: *Sound of rummaging around and things dropping to the floor.*

HAMMABLE: What *isn't* in here? Eye make-up. Combs. Brushes. Scarves. Lip gloss. Sunglasses. A pomegranate. A half-eaten sandwich.

SNEEZER: *(Hopefully)* Any Kleenex?

HAMMABLE: No.

SNEEZER: Any gold?

HAMMABLE: I'm looking! I'm looking! Wait! What's this?

SNEEZER: You tell me.

HAMMABLE: It's a golden wallet.

SNEEZER: There's something written on the side.

HAMMABLE: *(Reading)* "The Curse of the Purse awaits all who disturb the contents of the wallet within."

SNEEZER: Open it! We'll split the gold 50/50 and rule the Tunic world!

HAMMABLE: All right!

SOUND EFFECTS: *Thunderous crashing sound and a discordant chord of music.*

The Mummy's Purse

Coming back to the present . . .

Narrator #1: Back in Egypt, Dr. Butterball, Dr. Leafy and Charles Cartomb jump, startled.

Leafy: What happened? What *is* the curse?

Fufu: The curse is that anyone who disturbs the sacred wallet will be turned into a pillar of salt — except for me, of course.

Butterball: Salt?

Fufu: Look at the salt blocks over there!

Butterball: Those are . . . those are *people?*

Fufu: Sneezer and Hammable in the flesh . . . I mean, in the salt.

Butterball: What about the designs? Which one did you back, Carthage or Rome?

Fufu: Neither! We took the designs and ran all of them under *our* label. Calvin Kleinius and Armanius came and worked for me, and Egypt became the fashion leader of the world. Now . . . about that curse.

Butterball: Please — Will you spare our lives, Pharaoh Fufu?

Fufu: Oh, sure. Someone has to go set the records straight about the past. Let it be you. Now go and leave me in peace.

Butterball: Thank you for keeping us from becoming salt licks.

Cartomb: I will make certain that your tomb is never disturbed again.

Fufu: Thanks, Chuck.

Leafy: Oh, Pharaoh Fufu, before we go, um, uh, could you help me find something to wear that goes with my hair?

Fufu: Honey, I knew you were a fashion emergency when first I laid eyes on you. Here, sit down! This might take a while.

THE END

TEACHER INSTRUCTIONS

WHAT'S THE REAL STORY?

It is important that students understand that *The Mummy's Purse* twists facts and fantasy. However, many of the terms mentioned in *The Mummy's Purse* refer to, or are similar to, real historical events, people, places and things.

Have students find out the *real* story behind the items listed on page 27, "What's the REAL Story?" Depending upon your students and your classroom situation, try one of the following approaches:

- Have students individually research the various items, or a selection of the items.
- Divide the items up between different groups of students, and have them report their findings back to the class.
- Make it a contest. See how much of the "real" story students can uncover in one class period, using the Internet, encyclopedias, and other sources.

For your convenience, here is some basic information about each item:

PUNIC WARS: Wars that started in 264 B.C. between Rome and Carthage, for control in the western Mediterranean.

JULIUS CAESAR: Influential political and military leader of Rome. Caesar eventually became dictator, helping to establish the Roman Empire, but was assassinated in 44 B.C. by a group of conspiring senators, who feared he had too much power.

CLEOPATRA: Queen of Egypt, from 51 B.C. to 30 B.C. She committed suicide to avoid being put on display when Octavian conquered Alexandria. It was said that she was charismatic, intelligent, devoted and ruthless.

HANNIBAL: A great Carthaginian military leader who marched on Rome in the second Punic War (218-201 B.C.). He is famous for crossing the Alps in 15 days.

ROME: Present day capital city of Italy. It was the capital of the Roman Empire.

CARTHAGE: An ancient city on the northern coast of Africa. Rome defeated it in the 2nd century, B.C., following the Punic Wars.

PHARAOH: A king or ruler of ancient Egypt.

SPHINX: From Egyptian mythology, a figure having the body of a lion and the head of a man, ram or hawk. In Greek mythology, it is a winged monster with the head of a woman and the body of a lion.

HIEROGLYPHICS: A system of writing used in ancient Egypt. Figures and objects were used to represent sounds and words.

HATSHEPSUT: Queen of Egypt of the 18th dynasty, 1481-1540 B.C. She acquired power as no other queen before and had herself crowned a pharaoh.

Teacher Instructions, continued

What's the Real Story?

Papyrus: A kind of paper made from the pith and stems of a plant and used as an ancient writing material.

Nile: A river in eastern Africa. It is the longest river in the world.

Scribe: A professional copyist of manuscripts and documents.

Plebians: Members of early Roman lower classes.

Gaul: A term used to describe a region inhabited by the ancient Gauls. It was located south and west of the Rhine River, west of the Alps and north of the Pyrenees. The area is now modern-day France and parts of Belgium, western Germany, and northern Italy.

Apollo: In Greek mythology, the god of prophecy, music, medicine and poetry.

Soothsayer: A person or prophet who predicts future events.

Ur: An ancient city in Sumer, which is now southeastern Iraq.

Catacombs: Underground tunnels and passages used as cemeteries in early Rome. Niches or recesses in the walls were used as graves.

Crete: A Greek island in the Mediterranean.

Archaeologist: A person who scientifically studies material remains of past people and societies.

STUDENT INSTRUCTIONS

WHAT'S THE REAL STORY?

The Mummy's Purse is a play that twists history. However, many of the terms mentioned in the play refer to, or are similar to, real historical events, people, places and things.

Find out the *real* story behind the items listed below. Identify each with a short explanation.

PUNIC WARS

JULIUS CAESAR

CLEOPATRA

HANNIBAL

ROME

CARTHAGE

PHARAOH

SPHINX

HIEROGLYPHICS

HATSHEPSUT

PAPYRUS

NILE

SCRIBE

PLEBIANS

GAUL

APOLLO

SOOTHSAYER

UR

CATACOMBS

CRETE

ARCHAEOLOGIST

FOR YOUR INFORMATION...
MUMMIES

When most people hear the word mummy, they think of a stiff-legged, stiff-armed creature with old, white, unraveling bandages — the kind of mummies that we see in movies like "The Mummy" and cartoons like "Scooby Doo." However, the word "mummy" actually has a much broader meaning. It can apply to any person or animal who was preserved after death, either by accident or some intentional process.

THE BASIC MUMMY

Cultures and societies throughout history have practiced mummification, though ancient Egyptians are the most well-known. The word *mummy* usually refers to a body embalmed or treated for burial with preservatives. In Egypt, the process varied, but there were some standard mummification practices.

First of all, the internal organs were removed from the body. The lungs, stomach, liver and intestines were removed through an incision in the left side of the abdomen. Then the brain was taken out through the nose with a brain hook, which looked like a crochet needle. The heart was left in the body because it was considered the source of thought. After that, the body was rinsed with wine, which helped to kill any bacteria. Then the body was rubbed and packed in salt and left to dry for about 40 days.

After the drying of the body, it was ready to be restored. The restoration process was undertaken to make the body beautiful so that the spirit could find it. The skin of the corpse was massaged, and padding was slipped under the skin to round out the dried flesh. The body was stuffed and perfumed, and rouge and other paint was applied. Finally, the body was coated in warm resin and wrapped in about 150 yards of linen strips.

The entire practice of mummification was based on the belief that a person finds a new, eternal life after death. The body had to be mummified so that the dead's spirit would have a permanent home. Many steps were taken to ensure that the dead were well prepared for the afterlife. For example, in a "reanimation" ritual, Egyptians performed a ceremonial opening of the mouth. This was done to ensure that the mummy could eat and breathe in the next life. Egyptians also mummified animals to provide food for dead humans in the next life. Pets, like dogs and cats, were also preserved and buried with their owners so that the dead would have companionship on the other side. Mummies were also buried with furniture, jewelry, clothes or anything that might be useful to a person in the afterlife. Egyptians even visited the mummy tombs to bring food and other offerings to sustain the dead in the afterlife.

KING TUT

King Tut is probably the most famous mummy in history. His full name is King Tutankhamen. Even though King Tut is one of the most famous Egyptian kings today, he ruled for a very short time and did very little. He is so well known in modern times simply because of his tomb. His tomb is so remarkable to us today because it remained unaltered and completely intact until 1922, when it was discovered by Howard Carter, a British Egyptologist. The tomb had escaped plundering for thousands of years because many people didn't even know it existed.

A NEW MUMMY DISCOVERY

In the spring of 1999, a donkey stumbled upon a crumbling tomb in Egypt's Western Desert. This tomb surprised archaeologists because there were no pyramids or mausoleums nearby. However, it has turned into one of the largest ancient Egyptian cemeteries ever discovered. The mass graveyard covers over 1,250 square miles and holds as many as 10,000 mummies buried more than 2,000 years ago.

Experts say that the desert is a perfect place to house mummies because the dry climate helps to preserve the bodies. In the more humid regions of Egypt, many mummies have decomposed. In the vast desert, the tombs are easy to find because they are usually marked by slight depressions of loose sand in the ground.

This mass desert cemetery reminds us that kings weren't the only people mummified after death. Except for a 400-year period when only kings were preserved, every Egyptian had the right to become a mummy. Some of the recently discovered mummies clearly came from wealthy families because they were buried with golden masks. Other mummies are housed in simple terracotta coffins, merely coated in plaster or wrapped in linen.

MUMMIES FROM AROUND THE WORLD

While most people associate mummies with Egypt, mummies have been discovered in other areas of the world. In the late 1980s, ancient mummies were found buried in the Takla Makan Desert of China. The bodies were amazingly well preserved, basically freeze-dried by the desert air. Even though the mummies were found in China, they are not ancestors to the modern-day Chinese. Amazingly, these 4,000-year-old mummies have European features like long reddish-blond hair. Why these people lived in the heart of Asia 4,000 years ago and why their culture disappeared are two of the great mysteries of modern China.

In the fall of 1996, a few Peruvian ranchers found a mass of mummies in a forest in the Andes. These mummies, from a long-forgotten tribe called the Chachapoya, were well preserved despite the humid climate of the cloud-cover forest where they were discovered. Also in the Andes, the Incas mummified their dead until the Spanish outlawed the practice in the 1500s and 1600s. The Spanish ransacked many of the Incan burial sites for religious reasons and to take the gold often buried with the mummies. Therefore, few Incan mummies still exist.

In the four corners region of the American Southwest, the Anasazi also practiced mummification. Their mummies were wrapped in fur and leather blankets and housed inside caves and rock holes. Many of the Anasazi mummies were wearing new sandals to wear in the next life.

It's All in the Name

In *The Mummy's Purse*, many of the characters have silly names. The names, however, do more than make you chuckle. They also give you a hint about what the characters are like. For example, when you hear the name Julius Sneezer in the play, you immediately know that he is a comic character who has a sneezing problem. When you hear the name "Emperor Zero," you suspect that he may be something of a "loser."

Writers often use appropriate names to give readers a hint about what a character is like. Charles Dickens is quite famous for using character names such as Mr. Guppy, Mrs. Jellyby, Lady Deadlock, Mr. Krook and Mr. Nimrod.

Below is a list of short character sketches. For each character, come up with a name that tells us something about what the character is like.

_____ This man is in his late 30s, has no job and still lives with his parents. He spends his days lying on the couch watching soap operas and talk shows, while drinking orange Kool-Aid made with twice the sugar the recipe calls for. He wears the same jeans everyday with either his Beach Boy Reunion T-shirt or his "This is my lawn-mowing shirt" T-shirt.

_____ This teenaged girl only wears pink dresses with white lace. When she writes, she always dots her i's with hearts. She chews raspberry bubble gum and spends most of her time lying on her pink canopy bed dreaming about Ross from "Friends."

_____ This teenaged boy is very clean-cut. He secretly rakes leaves and mows his neighbors' lawns when they are gone. He gives all of his allowance away to charities, and spends his free time working at the homeless shelter. He never says anything negative, not even the word "no." He almost cries when he hears people say bad things about other people.

_____ This large woman is very jolly. She loves little kids and is always hugging them or pinching their cheeks. She spends her time in the kitchen whipping up spectacular desserts and baking dozens and dozens of cookies. She always says, "I always say: If God had intended me to be thin, he wouldn't have let me know the secret to the perfect pie crust."

Now invent a character of your own and write a one-paragraph character sketch. Be sure to name your character something that fits his or her personality.

THE IDIODYSSEY

THE IDIODYSSEY

CHARACTERS

DAN RATHERNOT. Host of the television show, "Take a Peek at History."
HOMER. Famous poet who wrote the *Iliad*, the *Odyssey* and other works.
APPLECLEESE. Leader of ancient Athens.
RIDICULES *(Ri-DIK-u-lees)* The greatest warrior in ancient Athens.
SALAMI. A soothsayer (one who can foretell events).
CASTOFF. Dulldrum's twin sister.
DULLDRUM. Castoff's twin sister.
POLYGRIP. Steerswoman for the *S.S. Minnow*.
LODESTAR. The lookout for the *S.S. Minnow*.
KING LAZYONE. Ruler of the island of Linoleum.
PRINCESS LULU. Daughter of King Lazyone.
POLYESTER. A sinister Cyclops.
SOUND EFFECTS. This "role" can be performed by a group of people. If the play is recorded as a radio show or performed in front of a group, the sound effects can be prepared carefully ahead of time.
If the play is read aloud in class, quick and easy methods of simulating sound effects should be improvised as the play is read. For example, the sound effects group might hum when music is specified, or drop books on a desk top when crashing noises are indicated.

SETTING: The set of a television program.

DAN RATHERNOT: Good evening and welcome to another edition of "Take a Peek at History." I am your host, Dan Rathernot. Tonight we will be visiting with one of the most famous poets of all time. I am referring, of course, to the honorable author Homer of ancient Greece. Please join me in welcoming him to our show.

SOUND EFFECT: *Applause.*

HOMER: Good evening.

Dan: Good evening. For those of you who aren't aware of the fact, Homer goes by only one name, just like Cher and Madonna and Sting. *(To Homer)*. We are just thrilled to have you with us tonight, sir. We are hoping that you will be willing to read us one of your excellent epic poems.

Homer: I don't read my poetry aloud. I'm blind.

Dan: Of course. My apologies. Will you *recite* one of your excellent epic poems then? Or *tell* us the story?

Homer: I would consider it a privilege.

Dan: Wonderful! Which one shall it be, the *Iliad* or the *Odyssey*?

Homer: I'm always asked to recite from those. I would prefer to relate one of my lesser-known works: the *Idiodyssey (id-ee-OD-u-see)*.

Dan: The *Idiodyssey*? I'm afraid I am not familiar with that one.

Homer: So much the better. Let me set the stage . . . In the dawn of Greek enlightenment, people lived in something called city-states. These city-states were in constant conflict with each other. The city-states of Athens and Sparta, in particular, were intense rivals.

Dan: I know they were involved in the Peloponnesian Wars in later years, around 431-404 B.C. Was this early rivalry as violent?

Homer: Not exactly. In the early days the city-states were more into practical jokes.

Dan: Excuse me, but did you say practical *jokes*?

Homer: Yes, the way I remember it, they would often raid each other's supplies of figs and dates and put hot sauce on them. One would order carryout from the olive gardens and force the other to pay for delivery. Frequently they would put bars of soap in each other's wine supplies . . . you know, the usual ancient world antics.

Dan: I see. I'm surprised these antics didn't result in warfare.

Homer: No. Instead Athens and Sparta resolved their differences in competitive games.

Dan: You mean they started the Olympics?

Homer: No, Mr. Rathernot. The games they started were different. They included competitions like a cannonball contest to see who could make the biggest splash into the Mediterranean. There was also a pelican pie-eating contest, thumb wrestling competitions, a goldfish swallowing event, and the most important event of all — the Colossal Crazy Eight Clash!

Dan: Colossal Crazy Eight Clash? What was that?

Homer: A card game.

Dan: A card game? The fate of the city-states rested on the results of a card game?

HOMER: Yes, and that is where the epic tale of the *Idiodyssey* begins.

DAN: *(Muttering)* It kind of sounds like we're in the middle of "idiodyssey" already!

HOMER: Let me begin my tale.

HOMER: *(Continuing)* The leader of Athens in those days was an intelligent, shrewd statesman named Applecleese. To ensure victory in the Colossal Crazy Eight Clash, he decided to send his greatest warrior, Ridicules *(ri-DIK-u-leez)* on a quest. It was a somber moment when Applecleese told Ridicules of his plans... Let's listen in...

GOING BACK IN TIME...

APPLECLEESE: Ridicules, my fine fellow, come. Sit. Oh dear, is that blood on your face? Are you hurt?

RIDICULES: No, my noble leader, Applecleese. The red comes from my pie-eating training.

APPLECLEESE: Here, take this towel and wipe off your face. I fear our ultimate victory over Sparta in these games is in grave doubt.

RIDICULES: Applecleese, how can you believe that? The pelican pie-eating contest will be a piece of cake for us. And the egg toss and the sack race will also be easy wins. Our victory is in the bag!

APPLECLEESE: Your confidence is inspiring. However, officials have determined that the outcome of these games will be decided in the *final* competition.

RIDICULES: You mean, the card game?

APPLECLEESE: Precisely, my boy — the Colossal Crazy Eight Clash. Furthermore, the gods from Mount Olympus have sent us a sign indicating how to ensure our triumph. Soothsayer Salami received an oracle while he was eating a pomegranate, which, you know, makes the oracle the genuine article. The message was clear that, in order to win, we must secure the Golden Sleeves.

RIDICULES: The Golden Sleeves? What are they?

APPLECLEESE: I'm just repeating the message, not explaining it. Soothsayer Salami, come over here. Repeat the message exactly as it was given to you.

SALAMI: Ahhooheeh! *(Chanting)* "Whosoever weareth the Golden Sleeves cannot loseth in any card game." *(Speaking)* I happen to know that the Golden Sleeves are located on the island of Lennox.

APPLECLEESE: Well, then, Ridicules, you must go on a quest to obtain the Golden Sleeves from the island of Lennox.

SALAMI: *(Closing eyes and holding hands up in the air.)* Uh oh! Incoming oracle! *(Chanting)* Beware! Beware! The Golden Sleeves are guarded by a slithering, savage serpent and the hideous cyclops Polyester, who never sleeps...

APPLECLEESE: Is that all?

SALAMI: Oh. (*Chanting*) Also, lay off the green grapes on Tuesdays. (*Speaking*) That's it.

RIDICULES: But, Applecleese, I have no ship.

APPLECLEESE: Rest easy, my boy. Fargo the shipbuilder has constructed a sturdy 50-oared vessel out of tall pines from Mount Onionpeel. The ship, the *S.S. Minnow*, is seaworthy of the gods themselves.

RIDICULES: But what about a crew?

APPLECLEESE: You will have reliable Salami here to guide you with his second sight. Two beautiful women will join you as well. They are the lovely Lemon twins, Castoff and Dulldrum, who have selected 50 of Athens' finest men and women for a crew.

RIDICULES: The Lemon twins?

APPLECLEESE: Here they are.

CASTOFF AND DULLDRUM: Hi, Ricidules. We're the lovely Lemon twins.

COMING BACK TO THE PRESENT . . .

DAN: *(Interrupting)* Wait a minute, Homer. I thought women were not considered citizens in ancient Greece. How could the lovely Lemon twins join Ridicules? How could women be part of the crew?

HOMER: You don't have to be a citizen to go on a boat trip, for heaven's sake. Now to continue with the tale, Ridicules and his crew endured a lot of turbulent sailing, due to Poseidon's dislike for Ridicules.

DAN: Poseidon?

HOMER: You know, the god of the sea.

DAN: Oh. He disliked Ridicules?

HOMER: Oh sure. That's because Ridicules always did his laundry in the Aegean Sea.

DAN: I see. I think.

HOMER: *(Continuing)* Now, imagine Polygrip, the woman steering the boat. She tried to maintain control as the merciless sea tossed the tiny ship. If not for the courage of the fearless crew the Minnow would be lost . . . Imagine Ridicules and his crew fighting the merciless sea . . .

SOUND EFFECTS: *Sound of howling wind and crashing waves.*

GOING BACK IN TIME . . .

RIDICULES: Man and woman the oars! Stroke! Stroke! Stroke!

Polygrip: Ridicules! Ridicules!

Ridicules: Yes, Polygrip, what is it?

Polygrip: I can't hold the tiller much longer.

Dulldrum: Where are the seasick pills? I think I'm going to be ill.

Castoff: Sorry, Dulldrum. I only packed sun screen.

Ridicules: Salami, why didn't you foresee this storm with your second sight?

Salami: I think Poseidon caused a poor connection.

Ridicules: Stroke! Stroke! Stroke!

Polygrip: Ridicules! Ridicules!

Ridicules: What is it now, Steersman Polygrip?

Polygrip: (*Insulted*) Excuse me. Steers*man?*

Ridicules: All right, all right. What is it, Steers*woman* Polygrip?

Polygrip: That's better. Sir, the tiller has slipped out. I fear we're going to flounder.

Dulldrum: Ugh! Don't mention food, especially flounder. I hate flounder!

Castoff: Oh, I don't know about that. If it's simmered in butter sauce . . .

Polygrip: Yes, yes. And with those little white potatoes.

Ridicules: Hey! Let's save the recipe critique for another time. We're sinking!

Lodestar: (*Calling, from a distance*) Ridicules! Ridicules!

Ridicules: Lodestar, come down from that crow's nest. We're floundering.

Lodestar: No, thanks. I'll stay up here. I hate flounder. I just wanted to let you know that there's land off the starboard bow.

Polygrip: Did she say there's a Starbucks off the bow?

Dulldrum: Boy, could I go for a cup of coffee.

Castoff: I'll have a cappuccino.

Ridicules: Everyone grab a hold of something! We're going to crash!

Sound Effect: *Terrible crash.*

Coming back to the present . . .

Homer: The ship crashed on the shores of an uncharted island. Half of the crew was lost in the storm, yet luck had not altogether abandoned the resolute Ridicules. He and what was left of his crew were saved by a beautiful bevy of water nymphs, who brought the crew to shore. The next morning, Ridicules and his crew awoke to discover a group of friendly guards, who took them to the palace of the island's ruler, King Lazyone.

DAN: King Lazyone?

HOMER: Yes, good fortune had smiled upon Ridicules. He and his crew were on the island of Linoleum, in the presence of King Lazyone of the Locust-Eaters.

DAN: Locust-eaters? Don't you mean *lotus*-eaters? Lotus, as in flowers?

HOMER: No, locust-eaters, as in the insects — chewy, with no bitter aftertaste.

DAN: I believe I understand why this is one of your lesser-known works . . .

HOMER: Let me continue. We next meet the crew on the island of Linoleum . . .

GOING BACK IN TIME . . .

KING LAZYONE: Ridicules, I trust that you have met my lovely daughter, Princess Lulu?

RIDICULES: I have indeed.

KING LAZYONE: And I trust that you and your crew are sufficiently refreshed?

RIDICULES: That we are, kind King Lazyone. We are overwhelmed by your generosity. However, we must make haste to obtain the Golden Sleeves from the island of Lennox. The fate of Athens lies in the balance.

KING LAZYONE: The repairs on your ship will be completed by morning. However, I must warn you about the peril involved in your efforts to secure the Golden Sleeves. The Golden Sleeves are guarded, night and day, by the sinister cyclops Polyester and his slithering serpent.

RIDICULES: How close are we to the island of Lennox?

KING LAZYONE: I'd say you're just a Hoot and a Holler away.

LODESTAR: A hoot and a holler? Is that some kind of distance?

KING LAZYONE: No, Hoot and a Holler are the Clapping Cliffs that guard Lennox, which lies about a half day's journey from here. To reach the island of Lennox, your ship must first get past the Clapping Cliffs. Princess Lulu, bring me a bag of wind. I will lend it to Ridicules.

RIDICULES: Oh, no. I can't take your windbag, King Lazyone.

PRINCESS LULU: Trust me. He's got plenty.

KING LAZYONE: Princess Lulu! That's enough from you, young lady. Here, Ridicules. Use this bag of wind to give your ship the extra push you will need to elude the Clapping Cliffs.

Princess Lulu: And here is a gift from the goddess Vizeena *(Vye-ZEEN-uh)* herself. This powerful potion must be kept in its urn and used only in the most dire emergency.

Ridicules: But for what purpose?

Princess Lulu: That will become clear at the proper hour.

King Lazyone: Sleep now, my friends. Rest easy in the knowledge that your ship will be ready when you awaken.

Princess Lulu: And we will wrap up some locusts in a doggy bag for you to take with you on your voyage.

Dulldrum: Oh goody! *(She samples one.)* Mmmmmmm. Tastes just like chicken . . .

Ridicules: At the break of dawn, I will take my courageous crew and set off for the island of Lennox and the precious prize we seek: the Golden Sleeves.

> **Sound Effects:** *Sound of sea gulls and waves breaking against the ship.*

Lodestar: *(On the S.S. Minnow)* Ridicules! Ridicules! We are approaching the Clapping Cliffs.

> **Sound Effects:** *A loud clapping sound.*

Ridicules: Ready the wind bag.

Dulldrum: *(Calling)* Salami, Ridicules wants you.

Ridicules: Not *that* wind bag. Bring the bag King Lazyone gave us.

Castoff: Here it is, Ridicules.

Ridicules: Open it and aim it towards our sail.

> **Sound Effects:** *A loud whistling noise.*

Polygrip: Whoa! What power! That blew us clear through the cliffs!

Dulldrum: Wow!

Ridicules: Drop anchor!

> **Sound Effects:** *A loud splash.*

Ridicules: *(Continuing)* Landing party, prepare to disembark. That swirling haze surrounds the island of Lennox.

Castoff: *(Stepping off the ship with the others)* It looks so dark and forbidding!

Polygrip: Owww! These stones hurt my feet!

Dulldrum: You should have worn your sandals. Salami told us Lennox was a rocky island.

RIDICULES: Salami, how close are we to the Golden Sleeves?

SALAMI: (*Chanting*) Aheeh! The Golden Sleeves hang in a hollow from the barren brambles near a banana tree.

CASTOFF: Sounds ap-*peal*-ing.

RIDICULES: (*In a hushed whisper*) Quiet everyone. There's a hollow right over there. This might be it. Salami, are we safe here?

SALAMI: (*Whispering*) Not to fear. We are on the upwind side of the cyclop's savage serpent. Its keen smelling skill shall not detect our scent.

SOUND EFFECTS: *Hissing sound.*

POLYESTER: (*In a booming voice*) Fee—fi—fo—freak! My snake does smell a greedy Greek!

RIDICULES: (*Sarcastically*) Your second sight is really smoking today, Salami.

DULLDRUM: Whoa! Look how big he is!

POLYESTER: Come out where I can see you, robbers. I have not dined on Greeks for many a month.

POLYGRIP: What a terrible fate to die as a blue-plate special to an ogre with one eye!

POLYESTER: Hey, I resent that remark! It isn't easy to get a job when you have only 20-zero vision. Now get over here where I can keep an eye on you.

CASTOFF: Please don't eat us, Mr. Polyester, sir.

DULLDRUM: I swear that we taste like seaweed.

POLYESTER: Hmmm . . . sushi!

RIDICULES: Wait! You really look tired, Polyester. Your eye is all bloodshot. Does it hurt? Is it often watery?

POLYESTER: Why, yes! You see, I do keep long hours.

RIDICULES: I believe we have just the thing for you. Castoff, bring that Grecian urn from King Lazyone.

POLYESTER: What's a Grecian urn?

DULLDRUM: Oh, about a dollar an hour. *(She laughs, but the others just groan.)*

CASTOFF: Here it is, Ridicules.

RIDICULES: Come here, Polyester. I think I have the solution for your eye trouble. Tilt your head way back.

POLYESTER: What is this liquid?

The Idiodyssey

Ridicules: It is a powerful potion from the goddess Vizeena herself. Use it to soothe your tired red eye.

Polyester: Ooooh! That feels so cool, so good. I can see clearly now; the pain is gone! I can see all obstacles in my way! How can I ever repay you?

Ridicules: Funny you should ask . . . I would be willing to let you have this entire urn in exchange for those Golden Sleeves over yonder.

Polyester: You're pulling my leg? You mean you'd trade that precious potion from Vizeena for those shabby sleeves?

Ridicules: But of course!

Polyester: Friend, you've got a deal.

All: Hurray!

> **Sound Effects:** *Triumphant music.*

Coming back to the present . . .

Homer: And that is how Ridicules acquired the Golden Sleeves.

Dan: And I suppose you're going to tell me now that he returned to Athens, wore the sleeves, and won the Olympics?

Homer: Well, not exactly.

Dan: What do you mean?

Homer: On the return voyage, Ridicules and his crew stopped on the isle of Crete, set up a riverboat gambling casino, and made a ton of money. They all went on to become wealthy tycoons.

Dan: I see. Well, thank you, Homer, for sharing your *Idiodyssey* with us. I must say your tale has a very appropriate title. And, ladies and gentlemen, thank you for listening in to tonight's show. Tune in next week as we travel back in time to ancient Mesopotamia to examine Hammurabi's zip code on another edition of "Take a Peek at History."

The end

Teacher Instructions

What's the REAL Story?

It is important that students understand that *The Idiodyssey* twists both history and mythology. With "What's the Real Story?" on page 45, they are reminded, or learn for the first time, about some of the terms, characters and events.

Have students find out the *real* story behind the items listed below. Depending upon your students and your classroom situation, try one of the following approaches:

- Have students individually research the various items, or a selection of the items.
- Divide the items up between different groups of students, and have them report their findings back to the class.
- Make it a contest. See how much of the "real" story students can uncover in one class period, using the Internet, encyclopedias, and other sources.
- Have students "untangle" the *Odyssey* myth from the myth of "Jason and the Argonauts." (Elements from both appear in *The Idiodyssey*. Which elements are from "Jason and the Argonauts?" Which are from the *Odyssey?*)

For your convenience, here is a quick background for each item:

HISTORICAL

HOMER. Classical Greek epic poet who is believed to have written the *Iliad* and the *Odyssey*.

THE *ILIAD*. An epic poem that outlines the events of the siege against Troy.

THE *ODYSSEY*. An epic poem that begins with the story of Odysseus' defeat of Troy, and the events that led him to become stranded on the island of Calypso.

A brief synopsis: Everyone thinks Odysseus is dead, but his son, Telemachus, sets out to seek news of his father's fate, hoping that he may still be alive. He visits Menelaus, who was in his father's army. He tells Telemachus where Odysseus is, and Zeus, the king of the gods, instructs Calypso to release him. Poseidon, in retaliation against Zeus, his long-time enemy, creates a fierce sea storm, which Odysseus barely survives.

Odysseus is washed ashore on the island of the Phaeacians. The king invites Odysseus to a banquet, where Odysseus is prompted to reveal his identity and tell of his adventures. Odysseus tells the tales of his journey, including his confrontation with the Cyclops, who ate some of his men; Circe, the enchantress who turned some of his men into pigs; the Sirens; the deadly whirlpool Charybdis; and the six-headed monster, Scylla. After his men braved these dangers, they arrived on the island of the Sun, where they disobeyed a warning by sacrificing cattle. In anger, Zeus destroyed Odysseus' ship with a thunderbolt, and only Odysseus survived, washed up on the island of Calypso.

After hearing of Odysseus' adventures, the king orders him to return home to Ithaca. He returns disguised as an old man, in order to discover who is still loyal to him.

Time Warped • Copyright © 2001 • Cottonwood Press, Inc. • 800-864-4297 • www.cottonwoodpress.com

Teacher instructions, continued

During his absence, suitors have been seeking to marry Penelope, his wife. At a feast one night, Penelope devises a test for the suitors: whoever can drive an arrow through twelve ax heads will get to marry her. All of the suitors fail, except Odysseus, whom everyone believes is a beggar.. Then, with the help of the goddess Athena, Telemachus, and two loyal herdsmen, Odysseus murders the suitors and the others in the household who betrayed him. Penelope, after doubting Odysseus' identity, finally rushes into his arms after she receives a secret sign that tells her it is her long lost husband.

PELOPONNESE. The southernmost geographic section of mainland Greece.

PELOPONNESIAN WAR. The war (431 – 404 B.C.) between the city-states of Athens and Sparta and their allies.

CITY-STATES. Independent, self-governing cities in ancient Greece. They were usually separated from other city-states by mountains or sea.

MOUNT OLYMPUS. Greece's highest mountain peak. In mythology, Mount Olympus was the home of the gods.

GRECIAN URN. A large clay pot decorated with mythological figures and/or classic Greek designs.

HAMMURABI. An 18th century B.C. Babylonian king who organized the first code of law.

AEGEAN SEA. an arm of the Mediterranean, located between the Greek peninsula and Turkey and bordered by Crete.

ATHENS. Greece's capital, considered to be the birthplace of Western civilization because of the number of artistic and intellectual ideas that originated and flourished there.

SPARTA. Ancient capital of southeastern Peloponnese. Sparta developed a rigid society that ignored the arts and instead created Greece's most powerful army.

MEDITERRANEAN SEA. The world's largest inland sea, located between Asia, Europe, and Africa.

MESOPOTAMIA. Greek for "between rivers," a culturally influential region located between the Tigris and Euphrates Rivers. The world's earliest civilization developed here around the end of the third millennium B.C.

PERICLES. A fifth century B.C. statesman who made Athens the political and cultural center of Greece.

MYTHOLOGICAL

JASON AND THE ARGONAUTS. A Greek myth that tells of Jason's adventures.

A brief synopsis: Jason, the unborn son of the king of Iolcus, in Thessaly, is the rightful heir to the throne. However, the king's half brother, Pelias, unjustly takes the throne and keeps the king a prisoner so he can't reveal the truth. Jason's mother, worried that Pelias will murder Jason at birth, tricks him by mourning as if Jason is dead and later takes him to a centaur called Chiron.

Chiron raises Jason, and when he comes of age, sends him out to claim his right to the throne. An oracle has warned Pelias of Jason's return to claim the throne, so when Jason arrives, he tricks him. He makes him believe that by retrieving the Golden Fleece he can prove his worthiness to be a hero and therefore, a king. Pelias hopes that by sending Jason on the quest for the Golden Fleece, he will perish.

Jason, being a true hero, gathers 50 men and sets out on the ship, the Argo. They first encounter Phineius, a king who is in danger of starving because Harpies, vulture-like creatures with the heads of women, are stealing his food. Jason and the Argonauts save Phineius, who in turn instructs them on how to pass safely through the Symplegades, or Clashing Cliffs.

The Argo reaches Colchis, the island where the Golden Fleece is guarded by Aeetes, who refuses to give up the Fleece until Jason passes a couple of tests. First he must yoke and plow a field using two fire-breathing bulls with brass hooves. Then he must plant dragon teeth and destroy the army of men that spring up from the soil. Medea, AEtes daughter, uses her sorcery to help Jason accomplish these tasks, and they escape with the Golden Fleece. The Argo begins its journey back to Thessaly, and Jason finally returns home to Thessaly, triumphant.

SYMPLEGADES: Known as the Clashing Rocks in Greek mythology, these rocky islands are located at the entrance to the Black Sea. In their search for the Golden Fleece, Jason and his Argonauts had to pass through them without being crushed.

THE LOTUS EATERS: In the *Odyssey*, Odysseus and his men come to the land of the lotus-eaters, who live on lotus flowers that they offer to some of the men. The lotus makes the men care less and less about returning home, and instead want to stay on the island and eat more lotus. Finally, Odysseus forces them to stop, and they escape from the island.

CYCLOPS: A giant, one-eyed creature Odysseus and his men encounter in the *Odyssey*.

POSEIDON: Greek god of the sea and of water and brother of Zeus.

ORACLE: A revelation or message from a medium believed to be in communication with a deity.

SOOTHSAYER: Someone who has the ability to see into the future and receive prophecies.

NYMPH: Mythological female goddesses or nature spirits.

OGRE: A giant in folklore who feeds on humans.

POLYPHEMOS: The name of the Cyclops that Odysseus blinded in the *Odyssey*.

WHAT'S THE REAL STORY?

Many of the terms mentioned in *The Idiodyssey* refer to, or are similar to, real historical events, people, places and things. Others are similar to characters and events from Greek mythology.

Some of these terms are listed below. Using encyclopedias, the Internet or other research tools, track down the *real* identity of each. Describe each in a sentence or two, using your own words.

HISTORICAL

HOMER

THE *ILIAD*

THE *ODYSSEY*

PELOPONNESE

PELOPONNESIAN WAR

CITY-STATES

MOUNT OLYMPUS

GRECIAN URN

HAMMURABI

AEGEAN SEA

ATHENS

SPARTA

MEDITERRANEAN SEA

MESOPOTAMIA

PERICLES

Student Instructions, continued

MYTHOLOGICAL

Jason and the Argonauts

Symplegades

The Lotus Eaters

Cyclops

Poseidon

Oracle

Soothsayer

Nymph

Ogre

Polyphemos

FOR YOUR INFORMATION

The play *The Idiodyessy* is a spoof of the *Odyssey*, a long epic poem that details the travels of Odysseus. Or is that Ulysses? Odysseus and Ulysses are actually the same mythological character. To ancient Greeks, the hero was Odysseus. To the Romans, he was Ulysses. Ancient Greeks and Romans shared many of the same gods in their mythology. However, to make it confusing, they all had different names.

You may be wondering how two different cultures could share the same religion, stories and gods. The truth is that the Romans "borrowed" their mythology from the Greeks. Ancient Romans were very thorough in their religious rituals, but they never really emphasized the moral element that was the foundation of their ceremonies. It was as if they practiced religion customs but they didn't really have a religion.

The Greeks, on the other hand, were quite different. They were deeply interested in the religion and its relationship with humanity. Through their stories and imaginations, the Greeks were able to bring their gods to life. They personalized them and made them almost human.

Here is a list of some mythological gods with both their Roman and Greek names.

Greek	**Roman**	**Designation**
Aphrodite	Venus	Goddess of Love and mother of Cupid/Eros
Ares	Mars	God of war
Artemis	Diana	Goddess of the harvest, nature and fertility
Athena	Minerva	Goddess of wisdom, war and the arts
Demeter	Ceres	Goddess of agriculture and grain
Dionysus	Bacchus	God of wine and drama
Eros	Cupid	God of love
Helios	Sol	God of the sun
Hephaestus	Vulcan	God of fire
Hera	Juno	Queen of the gods
Heracles	Hercules	Heroic mortal son of Zeus/Jupiter
Hermes	Mercury	God of trade, profit, merchants and tradesmen
Hestia	Vesta	Goddess of home and hearth
Odysseus	Ulysses	King of Ithaca and Greek warrior
Persephone	Prosperina	Goddess of the underworld and daughter of Ceres/Demeter
Poseidon	Neptune	God of the sea
Selene	Luna	Goddess of the moon
Zeus	Jupiter	Supreme god

Time Warped • Copyright © 2001 • Cottonwood Press, Inc. • 800-864-4297 • www.cottonwoodpress.com

Twisting History

The Idiodyssey twists history in many ways. One noticeable way is that the crew of the *S.S. Minnow* includes the Lemon twins, who are, of course, women. If *The Idiodyssey* were historically accurate, the Lemon twins would not even be allowed on the ship, much less be allowed to serve as part of the crew. Respectable women in Greek society were secluded in their homes. Wives were not even allowed to eat at the same table as their husbands and guests.

The lovely Lemon twins would most likely have been forced to marry whomever their parents chose, regardless of their own feelings. If they decided to date someone else, in some circumstances they might have been sold by their own father as slaves. Polygrip would have been managing her husband's household and trying to give birth to male heirs, not steering a ship.

Why didn't women vote to change all that? Women were forbidden to vote and, of course, couldn't get anywhere near a position of political power. This treatment of women is ironic, considering that ancient Greece was the first democracy. It was also known for promoting the dignity and nobility of the human being.

So much for a government by the people, for the people. It was more like a government by the men, for the men!

- Many people today still believe that the roles of men and women are not truly equal in U.S. society. Others say that the roles are equal in importance, just different. What do you think? How are boys and girls treated differently in our society? In schools? How are expectations different for boys and girls? What do these differences mean, in your opinion? Are they fair? Unfair? Explain.

- What does it mean to say that the treatment of women in ancient Greece is "ironic"? Judging from the use of the word in the second to last paragraph, above, what do you think "ironic" means?

- The Greeks promoted democracy, yet they weren't democratic in their treatment of women. In the modern world today, what are some differences between what is "said" and what "is"? Explain.

MYTHOLOGICAL MONSTERS

In the ancient world, monsters were commonplace in myths, legends and oral stories. Here is a list of some of the monsters of Greek mythology:

ARGUS. A monster with a hundred eyes. Hermes put him to sleep and cut off his head. Hera scattered the eyes in a peacock's tail.

CERBERUS. A three-headed dog that guarded the entrance to the underworld, called Hades.

CYCLOPS. A giant with one eye in the middle of his forehead.

GORGONS. Three sisters who were so ugly they could turn anyone who looked at them into stone. They had snakes for hair, bronze hands and golden wings.

HARPIES. Smelly monsters, half woman and half vulture. They tore at their victims with claws.

MINOTAUR. A monster with the head of a bull and the body of a man. It was kept in the Labyrinth, a maze-like building, and was said to feed on human flesh.

SIRENS. Sea nymphs, half woman and half bird, who lived on an island. Their singing lured sailors to their shores, where the men forgot home and friends and starved to death. Or, according to some accounts, the Sirens would pounce and rip the men apart.

Now it is your turn. See if you can create a mythological monster for modern times. To get started, answer the questions below.

- What special powers does your monster possess?
- Is your monster good or evil? What good or evil does it do?
- What makes your monster modern?
- What does your monster look like? Describe every detail.
- What is your monster's name?

Take your answers from above and write a paragraph or more about your monster. Based on your description, draw what your monster looks like.

EXTRA CHALLENGE

Write a short story or myth that involves your monster. Or make a comic book that tells a story or myth about your monster.

A Poem of Epic Proportions

The *Odyssey*, written by Homer, is an epic poem. An epic poem is a long narrative poem that tells of the exploits and travels of a great hero. Many epics are based on oral stories passed down from generation to generation through storytelling or song. The epics usually reflect the morals and values of the society that created them.

As you can probably imagine, writing a long poem that tells a story is not an easy thing to do. However, it can be a beautiful way to tell a story.

Directions

Join the ranks of Homer, John Milton and Henry Wadsworth Longfellow by writing an epic poem, but just a *mini* epic poem. Base your poem on a story you have heard before. Look at the list below for ideas:

- A bedtime story that your parents told you or read to you when you were younger
- A story you have heard in your church, synagogue, or other place of worship
- A story about your family or ancestors
- A story about a real-life, modern-day hero
- A ballad or love song that tells a story

Remember that the epic needs to be based only very *loosely* on something you have heard before. Poets are known for taking "poetic license"— in other words, sometimes changing details to make a better story.

Getting Started

Write the entire story down before you plunge into writing the actual poem. Go back over what you have written and cross out anything you don't want to include in your poem. Just as the masters did, include only what will contribute to making a good story.

Some questions to answer before you begin your poem:

- Who is the hero?
- Is there a villain? If so, who?
- What does the hero accomplish?
- Is there a love interest? Is this a romantic mini-epic? If so, explain.
- Is there any comic relief? If so, who or what is funny?
- How does the poem end? Is it sad, happy or humorous? What is the ending?

CONTINUED

Writing the Poem

Rhyming is one of the most important parts of an epic poem. The poems are often written in rhyming couplets, which are pairs of lines that rhyme. Here is an example:

It came from a place, far, far away —
A three-headed spider with feet made of clay.

Your mini-epic poem should include at least 20 rhyming couplets.

Remember that lines of poetry aren't usually very long — rarely more than about ten words. Take a look at some story poems and epics before you get started. Some examples: "The Cremation of Sam McGee," by Robert William Service, *Hiawatha* by Henry Wadsworth Longfellow, *The Highwayman*, by Alfred Noyes. To remind you to keep your lines short, fold your paper in half before you start writing your first draft.

THE SCHMIKINGS

THE SCHMIKINGS

CHARACTERS

NARRATOR #1
NARRATOR #2
SCHMIKINGS (male)
    GUNTHER THE BORE
    OLAF THE STOUT
    IVAN THE FRECKLED
    SVEN FORKBEARD
    HAGAAR (HAY-gar) HAIRY LEGS
SCHMIKINGS (female)
    ULGA THE SHY
    BRUNHILDA THE BOSSY
    HELGA THE SHORT
MORGACELLAFANE (Mor-guh-SELL-uh-fane). A female mystic.
JUMBUBBLE. A giant.
HARRY EYESORE. The mayor of the village of Glazingham.
VIKING VOICES. The voices of many Vikings. May be played by any number of people.
SOUND EFFECTS. This "role" can be performed by a group of people. If the play is recorded as a radio show or performed in front of a group, the sound effects can be prepared carefully ahead of time. If the play is read aloud in class, quick and easy methods of simulating sound effects should be improvised as the play is read. For example, the sound effects group might hum when music is specified, or drop books on a desk top when crashing noises are indicated.

SETTING: Long, long ago, in a land far away.

VIKING VOICES: (*Together*)
    We roam the waves in our dragon ships
    searching for plunder and gold.
    We're warriors so cruel who break every rule
    and conquer the world so bold.
    We're Vikings! We're Vikings! So vile, so rotten, so free!
    We're Vikings! We're Vikings! Cunning kings of the sea!

The Schmikings

Narrator #1: For 300 years, northern Europe lived in constant fear of a mighty marauding group of Scandinavian seafarers called the Vikings. These huge brawny men would appear out of the sea mist and pillage a village at will.

Narrator #2: Although most historians aren't aware of it, another band of brutish barbarians also existed at this time. These outcasts had been kicked out of the clan of regular Vikings because they were always getting seasick. They lived in seclusion, longing to be feared like their sailing brothers. They were . . . the *Schmikings*.

All Schmikings (*Together*):

We stroll the trails in our deerskin boots,
seeking adventure we lack.
We scale every hill, 'cause the sea makes us ill,
and we tend to go down the wrong track.
We're Schmikings! We're Schmikings! So somber and *sole*ful are we!
We're Schmikings! We're Schmikings! Nauseous when we're at sea!

Narrator #1: Yes, the sad and lonely group of Schmikings lived in the forests of northern Jutland. Shying away from the fjords and jagged coastline, they carved out a life through farming and hunting. And yet the burning desire to steal, pillage and destroy was constantly with them.

Narrator #2: When the Vikings needed to discuss problems and settle disputes, the leaders, known as Jarls *(Yarls)*, would hold an open-air meeting called a Thing. After many long years of despair, the Schmikings finally decided to call a Thing of their own . . .

Sound Effects: *Sound of pounding.*

Ivan: All right, all right. Let's get this Thing started. Olaf the Stout, put down that turkey leg.

Olaf: Hey, who died and made you Jarl, Ivan the Freckled?

Brunhilda: Don't talk with your mouth full, Olaf.

Olaf: Yes, Brunhilda the Bossy.

Hagaar: Let's have some order here!

Sound Effects: *Sound of spoon striking a bowl.*

Helga: If we're taking orders, I'd like some more wild boar stew then, Hagaar Hairy Legs.

Hagaar: Not *that* kind of order, Helga the Short. We've got to get organized.

Ivan: Hear, hear. Let us not argue. We must work together.

Olaf: Quite right. Speak then, Ivan the Freckled.

Ivan: The Viking raids upon England are constantly increasing. We must act swiftly or all the good villages will be destroyed. Then we won't have a chance to destroy one ourselves!

Brunhilda: This is true, Ivan, but how do you propose we get over there? Only the Viking ships can cross the North Sea.

Gunther: Yes, and we all know that if we got in a ship, we would be hanging our heads over the rail of the boat before it even left the dock.

Hagaar: I still think my idea of the catapult could work.

Helga: Are you crazy, Hagaar? Our friend Bjorn Ironsides didn't even make it halfway across last time.

Brunhilda: And now his soul will forever rest uneasy, as he has gone to the Shore of the Corpses.

Hagaar: Is that bad?

Brunhilda: It's a terrible place! It's one of the levels of the vast, cold realm of death. On that particular level, the serpent Nidhogg eats corpses!

Ivan: Well, the rest of us will never ride the burial ships to the great hall Valhalla if we continue to live like this.

Hagaar: Valhalla? Is that a place we *want* to go?

Brunhilda: Yes. Can't you remember anything? Valhalla is on Asgard, the home of the gods.

Gunther: Valhalla is the hall of slain warriors. They live there, blissfully happy.

Ulga: It's a wonderful palace, and the warriors feast every day on the flesh of a boar that is made whole again every single night.

Helga: I want to go to Valhalla!

Brunhilda: But Ulga the Shy, don't you have to be *dead* to go?

Ivan: We want to go there *eventually*, but to do that we have to prove our courage in battle and save everyone here in our town of Hideho *(HIDE-ee-ho)* from the Vikings.

Olaf: Hey, didn't we prove our courage with those raids last month on the honey trees and squirrel nests?

Gunther: Yes, those were pretty scary!

Helga: Those raids represented our little town of Hideho quite well, if you ask me.

Ulga: Nobody asked you.

Brunhilda: Those don't count as fearless raids, you fools. Everyone in our town of Hideho will go straight to the Shore of Corpses unless we do better than that. We women are counting on you men!

IVAN: Brunhilda is right. Lord Odin, our god of war, will be impressed with us only if we are as barbaric as the Vikings. We need a good raid on some Anglo-Saxon people in England. Ulga, where is Sven Forkbeard?

ULGA: Ivan, he went to the Savage Forest early this morning.

IVAN: Is he hunting again?

HAGAAR: I hope he got another wild boar. Those boar burgers were good last week.

SOUND EFFECTS: *Sound of a door opening.*

SVEN: Here I am, Ivan. I was hunting, but for much bigger game this time than wild boar.

OLAF: That's all right. We have a wild *bore* here with Gunther already.

GUNTHER: Watch it, Olaf the Stout Stomach!

OLAF: Hey! Don't insult my stomach! Do you want a piece of me, Gunther? Right here? Right now?

SOUND EFFECTS: *Sound of a scuffle.*

IVAN: Silence! We will solve nothing quarreling among ourselves. Why did you enter the Forest Savage, Sven?

SVEN: Since we are out of ideas for how to compete with the Vikings and win, I have sought out the only person who can help us solve our dilemma.

GUNTHER: (*Shocked*) Gasp! You don't mean . . .

SVEN: Yes. Morgacellafane *(morg-uh-CELL-uh-fane)* the Mystic!

SOUND EFFECTS: *Sinister music.*

HELGA: (*Frightened*) Not Morgacellafane! She is evil.

GUNTHER: She will seal our doom.

SVEN: No. Morgacellafane has the second sight that can guide us over the North Sea.

IVAN: Did you find her?

SVEN: Yes, she is right outside. But you know she may not enter unless we all invite her in.

ULGA: Forget it!

BRUNHILDA: We might as well invite the Frost Giants of Utgard to enter, too!

HELGA: Beware! Evil follows her everywhere!

IVAN: Sven is right. We are at our wits' end here!

OLAF: Except for Gunther. He's at his half wit's end!

GUNTHER: All right! That's it! Put 'em up, Stout Boy! Put 'em up!

SOUND EFFECTS: *Sound of scuffle.*

IVAN: Break it up! Pull them apart! Save your rage for the raid.

HAGAAR: If we ever get a raid.

SVEN: Come on now! Are we all in agreement to invite the mystic in?

IVAN: All in favor say "Aye."

ALL except BRUNHILDA: Aye!

IVAN: Brunhilda, I didn't hear an "Aye" out of you.

BRUNHILDA: Oh, all right. I guess it is our only hope when you nitwits are at your wit's end.

SVEN: *(Calling)* Morgacellafane, we bid thee an invitation to ENTER!

SOUND EFFECTS: *Sound of door opening.*

MORGACELLAFANE: *(Entering)* Well, it's about time! I'm freezing my nose and toes off out here. *(She looks around at the group.)* Whoa! So these are the "Chickens of the Sea," huh?

OLAF: Hey, watch it!

MORGACELLAFANE: Listen. You all invited me in here.

IVAN: We are sorry, oh powerful mystic one. Has Sven Forkbeard explained our problem to you?

MORGACELLAFANE: Yes, yes. He told me all about it. You wild men of Hideho want to be barbaric, but you get too seasick to sail over to England.

ULGA: That's about it in a nutshell.

IVAN: Do you think you can help us?

MORGACELLAFANE: I don't know. Let's see. Do you have a cauldron filled with wild boar stew?

HELGA: Why, yes. Are you going to peer into it and foresee our future?

MORGACELLAFANE: No, I'm going to dip into it and feed my face. I'll foresee your future here in my crystal ball. Now get me a bowl of stew and dim the lights.

SOUND EFFECTS: *Sound of chair moving back. Then an ominous humming begins.*

GUNTHER: Gasp! Look at her crystal ball. It's glowing!

BRUNHILDA: Beware! It's evil!

MORGACELLAFANE: Nah. Those are only fireflies. Nice effect, isn't it?

SVEN: Do you see anything?

MORGACELLAFANE: Not yet. *(Chanting)* Odin! Odin! Odin! Send me a sign of how to help these people. Ah! I see — I see.

IVAN: What do you see?

MORGACELLAFANE: The Valkyries *(VAL-ku-reez)* themselves are sending me a sign . . .

HAGAAR: Who are the Valkyries?

ULGA: Are you so ignorant of Norse mythology? Valkyries are maidens who serve the god Odin. They go to the battlefield to pick which slain warriors should go to Valhalla.

MORGACELLAFANE: The sign . . . the sign. *(She chants.)*

A small town on the southern shore.
Defeating it will be no chore.
The English village of Glazingham
will soon be in an awful jam.
With no weapons, they can't defend . . .
The Schmiking folks will be their end!

OLAF: Schmiking *folks?* You mean *men.* Only Schmiking men do the raiding.

MORGACELLAFANE: *(Still chanting)*

The success of your raid will not be sure —
unless your *women* give the final cure.

SVEN: All right, they can come. But the men get to choose the trails!

IVAN: And we're not stopping to ask directions.

OLAF: But the village is in England. How can we get there?

GUNTHER: It cannot be by sea!

HAGAAR: Is it by air?

IVAN: Is there some kind of bridge?

MORGACELLAFANE: *(Still chanting)*

Not by land or air or sea
will your travels go.

You will find that "through the earth"
will make your fortunes grow.

SVEN: Through the earth? How can that be?

MORGACELLAFANE: *(Still chanting)*

On the northern tip of France there starts
the Chunnel that runs to English hearts.

HELGA: A Chunnel? Don't you mean tunnel?

MORGACELLAFANE: It is a tunnel that runs under the Channel between the two lands.

HELGA: We've never heard of that before. And how do we get from here to northern France?

SVEN: Can you guide us there, oh mystic one!

MORGACELLAFANE: For a cut of your take and another bowl of your stew, hey, let's talk business!

NARRATOR #1: So guided by the mystic Morgacellafane, the Schmikings were led on their adventurous passage from Norway, through Sweden, Denmark, Germany and the Netherlands and Belgium, to northern France. There they found the hidden entrance to the Chunnel.

NARRATOR #2 However, as they tried to enter, they were stopped cold by Jumbubble the Giant, who blocked their way.

JUMBUBBLE: Halt! Jumbubble the Giant orders thee to halt!

SOUND EFFECTS: *Sound of a toll booth bell ringing.*

BRUNHILDA: Oh great. A toll booth!

OLAF: Let's attack him.

SOUND EFFECTS: *Sound of sword banging on a shield.*

MORGACELLAFANE: No, wait. Only he holds the key to the passageway.

JUMBUBBLE:

People can't enter the Chunnel gateway for free,
unless they solve "The Riddle" for me!

SVEN: Speak then! Speak the riddle, oh mighty giant Jumbubble!

JUMBUBBLE:

They serve you well with an awful smell
and bark the whole night long.

They grow the corn when used at morn
and blister to the sun's harsh song!

ULGA: What kind of a riddle is that?

HELGA: A rotten one.

OLAF: Oh, oh, I know! I know! The answer is a wild boar!

JUMBUBBLE: Wrong, plump warrior.

HELGA: A wild boar? How did you come up with that?

HAGAAR: Well, it smells and eats corn and barks at night.

SVEN: It doesn't blister to the sun's harsh song. Morgacellafane, can't you find the answer with your crystal ball?

MORGACELLAFANE: No, my fireflies are not good with riddles.

BRUNHILDA: Oh, let me sit down. My feet are aching.

JUMBUBBLE: What did you say?

BRUNHILDA: They ache! My feet! My feet!

JUMBUBBLE: That is correct. You have solved my riddle.

SVEN: What?

JUMBUBBLE: The answer to the riddle is "Your feet."

BRUNHILDA: But I don't get it. My feet don't bark.

ULGA: I think it's an old saying. After a whole day in high heels, my grandma used to say, "My old dogs sure are barking."

BRUNHILDA: Ha! I knew it all the time.

JUMBUBBLE: Brilliant woman, you and your friends may use the Chunnel!

SOUND EFFECTS: *Sound of footsteps on a path.*

NARRATOR #1: The Schmikings followed the path of the Chunnel, untouched by the waters above. Upon reaching the other side they caught their first glimpse of the peaceful village of Glazingham.

SOUND EFFECTS: *The footsteps get louder and then fade as Ivan begins speaking.*

IVAN: There it is! At last, we shall pillage and destroy a village. Please, please Lord Odin, make our reservations on the ship to Valhalla.

SVEN: Hey, look. What's that?

GUNTHER: It's a Viking ship! The Vikings are also attacking Glazingham.

OLAF: *(Calling out)* Hey, back off, Bozos! We were here first!

IVAN: They're sending out their beserkers to engage the battle.

HAGAAR: What are berserkers?

SVEN: They are those guys dressed in animal skins. They are particularly savage warriors.

ULGA: Yes, where do you think the term "going berserk" comes from?

OLAF: Well, I'll beserk them! Ahhhh!

> **SOUND EFFECTS:** *Sound of swords clashing and people fighting.*

NARRATOR #2: The Schmikings do not want to lose the opportunity to prove themselves worthy of Lord Odin. They bravely fight against the marauding Vikings throughout the day. Finally, as the last rays of daylight leave the sky, the defeated Vikings set sail in their ship, never to bother the small village of Glazingham again.

> **SOUND EFFECTS:** *Sound of cheers.*

NARRATOR #1: *(Continuing)* The joyous villagers crowd around to crown the Schmikings the heroes of the day.

> **SOUND EFFECTS:** *More cheering, which fades as Eyesore begins speaking.*

EYESORE: Brave warriors, a thousand blessings be yours.

IVAN: Who are you?

EYESORE: My name is Harry Eyesore, mayor of this happy hamlet called Glazingham Ballads shall be written about your bravery in saving our town. Come! Allow us to hold a grand feast in your honor.

OLAF: Do you have any wild boar burgers?

EYESORE: Why, my friend, we are the Hog Capital of all England.

HELGA: You mean, you're wealthy?

EYESORE: Extremely so! Please consider our purse yours.

OLAF: Good. After we eat, we'll pillage and destroy this place.

> **SOUND EFFECTS:** *Humming sound begins and continues as Morgacellafane speaks.*

MORGACELLAFANE: Wait! There's a message coming through my crystal ball. It's the Valkyries:

Spare this village, my Schmiking friend,
and Odin's favor shall never end.

SVEN: Then we have pleased Lord Odin just by saving this village? How ironic! We were trying to please him by *destroying* the village!

IVAN: Schmikings, what say you all to staying and making this hamlet, and all its wealth, our own hometown. All in favor say "Aye."

ALL TOGETHER *(Except Brunhilda)*: Aye!

IVAN: Brunhilda, I didn't hear an "Aye" out of you.

BRUNHILDA: *(Mumbling)* Hey, this boar burger is great, and I never talk with my mouth full.

NARRATOR #1: For the Schmikings their wandering days came to an end in peace and prosperity. They lived their remaining days in the happy hamlet of Glazingham.

NARRATOR #2: And after a tidy number of years, the Valkyries escorted them to the hallowed hall of Valhalla in Asgard.

SCHMIKINGS: *(Together)*
We spared the village from the Viking fury
and found our adventure so grand!
The violence will cease as we live in peace
and own a huge slice of the land!
We're Schmikings! We're Schmikings! So wealthy and rich are we!
We're Schmikings! We're Schmikings! Odin's chosen chickens of the sea!

THE END

TEACHER INSTRUCTIONS

WHAT'S THE REAL STORY?

It is important that students understand that *The Schmikings* twists facts and fantasy. However, many of the terms mentioned in *The Schmikings* refer to, or are similar to, real historical events, people, places and things.

Have students find out the *real* story behind the items listed on page 66. Depending upon your students and your classroom situation, try one of the following approaches:

- Have students individually research the various items, or a selection of the items.
- Divide the items up between different groups of students, and have them report their findings back to the class.
- Make it a contest. See how much of the "real" story students can uncover in one class period, using the Internet, encyclopedias, and other sources.

For your convenience, here is a quick background for each item:

HISTORICAL

VIKINGS. Mariners and traders from Scandinavia (Norway, Sweden and Denmark) who attacked and colonized parts of Europe between the 8th and 11th centuries.

FJORDS. Long, deep narrow coastal inlets reaching far inland, mostly found in Norway, Greenland and Alaska.

NORTH SEA. A part of the Atlantic Ocean bordered by Britain, Norway, Belgium, Germany and Denmark.

ENGLISH CHANNEL. Body of water between England and France, connected to the North Sea.

JUTLAND. A northern European peninsula that includes mainland Denmark.

JARL. A medieval Scandinavian chieftain.

ANGLO-SAXON. A term used to define Angles, Saxons and Jutes, the people who settled in Britain in the fifth and sixth centuries.

MYTHOLOGICAL

ODIN. In Norse mythology, the supreme god and father of all gods.

NASTROND. Known as the Shore of Corpses, it is where Nidhogg exists.

VALHALLA. A great hall built by Odin to enshrine the souls of slain warriors.

NIDHOGG. Norse serpent who eats corpses and gnaws on the roots of the World Tree.

ASGARD. A heavenly place created by Odin to be the home of the gods.

UTGARD. Home of the frost giants and the rock giants.

VALKYRIES. Handmaidens of Odin who bring the souls of dead warriors to Valhalla.

Time Warped • Copyright © 2001 • Cottonwood Press, Inc. • 800-864-4297 • www.cottonwoodpress.com

STUDENT INSTRUCTIONS

WHAT'S THE REAL STORY?

Many of the terms mentioned in *The Schmikings* refer to, or are similar to, real historical events, people, places and things. Others are similar to characters and places from Norse mythology.

Some of these terms are listed below. Using encyclopedias, the Internet or other research tools, track down the *real* identity of each. Describe each in a sentence or two, using your own words.

HISTORICAL

VIKINGS

FJORDS

NORTH SEA

ENGLISH CHANNEL

JUTLAND

JARL

ANGLO-SAXON

MYTHOLOGICAL

ODIN

NASTROND

VALHALLA

NIDHOGG

ASGARD

UTGARD

VALKYRIES

FOR YOUR INFORMATION

Norse mythology refers to the collective myths of Scandinavia (Sweden, Denmark, Norway, and Iceland). The *Prose Edda* (c. 1220) and the *Poetic Edda* (c. 1270) tell us most of what we know about Norse mythology.

THE CREATION MYTH

The creation of the Norse universe began with a giant named Ymir. The giant was created from poisonous droplets of water from a stormy river. The giant's legs conceived a six-headed son, and a young woman and man were born from the giant's underarms. The giant Ymir was joined by a cow named Aughumla, created from the droplets of melted ice crystals.

Aughumla fed Ymir by creating four rivers of milk. She also created a man, Buri, by licking a salty stone until it was the shape of a man. Buri was the grandfather of Odin, who eventually was considered king of the gods, and his brothers.

Odin and his brothers killed the giant Ymir. Then the giant's body formed the earth. His bones are the rocks, his skull is the sky, his blood is the sea, his hair is the trees and his brains are the clouds.

The universe in Norse mythology centers around the Yggdrasill, also called the World Tree. This tree connects and shelters all of the worlds — Asgard, Jotunheim and Niflheim. Three springs lie at the foot of the World Tree, including the Well of Wisdom. Four deer run across the branches of the tree and nibble at its leaves, while the serpent Nidhogg gnaws at its roots. On the day of Ragnorok (the Norse armageddon), the tree will be destroyed by fire.

THE NORSE GODS

- ODIN is considered the father of the gods. Like many pagan gods, Odin is made up of both good and evil. While he is considered the god of war and death, he is also the god of poetry and wisdom. Several times, Odin sacrificed himself to gain knowledge. In return for a drink from the Well of Wisdom, Odin traded his eye for the knowledge from the well. Another time, Odin hanged himself from the World Tree. He pierced himself to the tree and hanged for nine days so that he could master the wisdom of magic and spells. His castle Valhalla is where slain soldiers live in eternal bliss.

    Odin carries his sword Gungnir and rides an eight-footed horse Slepnir. He is always seen with his two wolves, Freki and Geri. Odin survives by drinking only wine and gives all of his food to his two wolves. Odin's one eye blazes like the sun. Odin can also change shape at will and travel to other worlds.

- THOR is another well-known Norse god. He is the son of Odin and was worshiped by the Norse more than any other god. Scholars believe that Thor was more popular than his father because he did not require human sacrifice. Thor is the god of thunder, which he creates by riding his goat-drawn chariot through the heavens. He creates lightning by throwing his hammer. Thor also uses his hammer to smash the skulls of his enemies. A large, powerful man with a red beard and eyes of lightning, Thor is considered the champion and protector of the gods and humans. He is also responsible for the rains, which make him very popular with farming peasants. The day Thursday is named after Thor.

DWARFS

Dwarfs play an interesting part in Norse mythology. They began as maggots on the flesh of the slain giant Ymir. Considered wise craftsman, they forged the treasures of the gods, like Thor's hammer. Four dwarfs hold up the sky, which is made up of Ymir's skull. They live in mountain caves and are mostly friendly to humans.

SACRIFICE

Sacrifice was an integral part of worship for Norse pagans. They often sacrificed cattle and then sprinkled the blood and ate the meat of the sacrificed animal. Every nine years, they held a great festival where animals and humans were sacrificed. Like the god Odin, the sacrificed were hanged from a tree in the sacred grove.

THE AFTERLIFE

The Norse interpretation of the afterlife is generally dismal. Some believed that fallen warriors found eternal bliss in Odin's Hall of Valhalla. Most believed that the dead slowly passed through to Niflheim, an icy, cold and dark world.

Niflheim is the lowest level in the Norse universe. It includes Helhiem and Nastrond, the Shore of Corpses. On Nastrond, the serpent Nidhogg eats corpses and gnaws on the roots of the World Tree.

RAGNAROK

Ragnorak is the end of the world, according to Norse mythology. The myth describes Ragnarok as being preceded by the winter of winter, when humans will feud with each other, and all morality will be lost. The winter will be the beginning of the end.

The world will be plunged into total darkness after the wolf Skoll devours the sun and his brother Hati consumes the moon. The stars will also vanish. Giants and other monsters will attack the gods and humans. All the gods, including Odin and Thor, will be killed. The fire giant Surt will scorch the earth and destroy the World Tree with fire.

After everything is destroyed, the earth will sink back into the sea. Eventually a purified and renewed earth will rise, full of abundance and wealth. Humans deemed worthy will live forever in a hall of gold. Wickedness and misery will be gone forever, and gods and humans will live happily ever after.

Riddle Me This

In the play, the Schmikings are asked to solve a riddle. Solving riddles can be hard, but writing riddles can even be harder. Below are answers to riddles. Write a riddle to go along with each answer. Remember that your riddles need to rhyme, like the ones in the play. Here are some examples to help you get started:

ANSWER: BLUE
RIDDLE:
It's what makes the friendly skies
And is essential to Levis
It makes the ocean and the sea
and Brad Pitt's eyes dream-y

ANSWER: ROCK 'N' ROLL
RIDDLE:
Includes Britney and Macy
and the infamous Slim Shady
Parents start glaring
when it is blaring.

ANSWER: ENGLISH CLASS
RIDDLE:
Poe and Shakespeare
continually reside here
amongst gerunds and verbs
and vocabulary words.

ANSWER: BASEBALL
RIDDLE:
Its diamond does not shine
but it has a foul line
and a group of nine who scratch and spit
and wait on deck to try to hit.

BALLADS

At the end of *The Schmikings*, Mayor Eyesore of Glazingham says, "Ballads shall be written about your bravery in saving our town." A ballad is a song that tells a story. Ballads were very popular during the Middle Ages. However, they were much more than just songs. They were also a way for people who could not read or write to share stories and pass them down from generation to generation.

Some of the more popular ballads of medieval England told the stories of Robin Hood. Here are a few lines from one of the ballads:

Some cried, "Blue jacket!" Another cried, "Brown!"
And the third cried, "Brave Yellow!"
But the fourth man said, "Yonder man in red
In this place has no fellow."

For that was Robin Hood himself,
For he was clothed in red;
At every shot the prize he got,
For he was both sure and a dead shot.

So the arrow with the golden head
And shaft of silver white
Brave Robin Hood won, and bore with him
For his own proper right.

These outlaws there, that very day,
To stop all kind of doubt,
By three or four, no less no more,
As they went in, came out.

YOUR TURN

Try your hand at writing a ballad. Because ballads always tell a story, it is a good idea to start with a story that you already know. Here are a few ideas:

- a story about a historical event (*Battles are always popular.*)
- a love story (*Many ballads have been written about tragic love stories, like the story of Romeo and Juliet*)
- the adventures or trials of a hero (*Think of Olympic athletes, war heroes, great religious leaders or historical figures.*)

REFERENCES ON BALLADS

There are many sites on the Internet that list ballad lyrics. Here are a few:

- www.contemplator.com
- www.dnaco.net/~aleed/ballad/index.html
- www.legends.dm.net/ballads/

During the 1960s and 70s, musicians recorded modern-day versions of old ballads. Here are some examples you may want to listen to:

- Grateful Dead, "Jack-A-Roe"
- Bob Dylan, "Barbara Allen"
- Joan Baez, "Geordie"
- Simon and Garfunkel, "Scarborough Fair"

Many English poets turned old English ballads into literary poems. Here are a few titles:

- *The Lady of Shallot*, Alfred, Lord Tennyson
- *La Belle Dame Sans Merci*, John Keats
- *The Rime of the Ancient Mariner*, Samuel Taylor Coleridge
- *Goody Blake and Harry Gill*, William Wordsworth

- a moral lesson *(Think of stories from religious works or Aesop's fables, for example.)*
- a story from a movie or television special *(Some cartoon movies and historical movies actually had their start as ballads! You can base your ballad around any good plot.)*

SUMMARIZE

Before you plunge into actually writing a ballad, write a short summary of the story you are telling. While writing your summary, remember that you don't have to include every element of the story in your ballad. Pick and choose the bits and pieces that seem most important and most interesting.

Next, take your summary and turn it into a short outline of your ballad. Since you will be writing a 10 stanza ballad, include at least 10 points in your outline — one for each stanza. This will help you organize and write your ballad.

WRITING

Ballads are meant to be sung. Don't worry. You don't need to be an accomplished musician to write a ballad. Historically, ballads have been written to the tunes of existing songs. That made it easier for people to remember the songs.

First, you need to select an easy tune for your ballad, something well known, such as "Hush, Little Baby," "I've Been Working on the Railroad," "My Darling Clementine," "My Country 'Tis of Thee," "The Ballad of the Green Beret," etc. Once you have selected a tune for your ballad, the tune will also set the rhythm of your ballad.

You will need to include at least 10 stanzas in your ballad. You can also choose to have a refrain — a stanza that repeats throughout your song. Remember also that most ballads rhyme. For extra help with this, consult a rhyming dictionary.

BEGINNING AND ENDING

It is important that every ballad have a clear beginning and strong ending. Begin by writing the first and last stanza of your ballad. Then you can go back and fill in the meat of your story. Remember to use your outline to keep you organized.

There's No Ages Like Dark Ages

There's No Ages Like Dark Ages

CHARACTERS

Narrator #1
Narrator #2
Narrator #3
Narrator #4
Lord Morebred (MORE-bread): A nobleman who owns the manor Toadfat.
First peasant
Second peasant
Third peasant
Fourth peasant
Wizard Morrie: Lord Morebred's advisor.
Sheriff Rottingwood: the sheriff of the manor Toadfat.
Sara Lee Antoinette: a door-to-door saleswoman.
Clem Squiggly: a farmer.
Snarzdan: a female dragon.
Puff: the dragon Snarzdan's daughter.
Sound Effects. This "role" can be performed by a group of people. If the play is recorded as a radio show or performed in front of a group, the sound effects can be prepared carefully ahead of time. If the play is read aloud in class, quick and easy methods of simulating sound effects should be improvised as the play is read. For example, the sound effects group might hum when music is specified, or drop books on a desk top when crashing noises are indicated.

Setting: Many, many years ago in a kingdom far, far away.

Narrator #1:
Come lend an ear and you shall hear
a legend of Dark Ages long, long ago.

Narrator #2:
A feudalistic rule so vile and so cruel
melted freedom like flakes of snow.

There's No Ages Like Dark Ages . . .

NARRATOR #3:
Barbarian raids made folks afraid,
and protection was a necessity.

NARRATOR #4:
So manors existed in England's mists, and
nobles owned all the property.

NARRATOR #1:
Our tale so rare begins at a fair
in the burg of downtown Toadfat.

NARRATOR #2:
The peasants are mad, for things are bad.
They want their problems looked at.

PEASANTS: *(All together)* Morebred! Morebred! Morebred! We want Lord Morebred!

LORD MOREBRED: Peace! Peace! Be peaceful, I beg of you, my fine peasant people.

FIRST PEASANT: Lord Morebred, how dare you beg our peace when you have made a mockery of our lives?

SECOND PEASANT: Forsooth and for sure. That dreaded dragon, Snarzdan, has been wreaking havoc on our land.

THIRD PEASANT: Aye! Its fiery breath has terrified us all for 40 days and 40 nights.

FOURTH PEASANT: It singed the hair right off my Uncle Leo's head!

MOREBRED: Please let me speak! A day has not passed that I have not felt your pain. Were they not *my* fields and crops that burned as well? You speak as though I myself invited that wicked worm Snarzdan onto our land.

SECOND PEASANT: But, Lord Morebred, you are our lord high mayor. We turn to you for hope. Is there nothing that can be done to rid our land of this vile viper, Snarzdan?

MOREBRED: I'm working on it! I'm working on it! Where is my advisor, the Wizard Morrie?

MORRIE: I am here, my lord.

MOREBRED: Good. How many pazoozas (*puh-ZOO-zuhs*) have we got in the castle coffer?

MORRIE: Your lordship, our castle savings have been thoroughly exhausted.

THIRD PEASANT: How about our knights? How many of those are left?

MOREBRED: Alas, that slippery sinister Snarzdan has wiped out all of the knights of my square table already. Sir Dancelot was our last hope. I shall miss his two-step.

FOURTH PEASANT: Hey, what about getting Sheriff Rottingwood to help with Snarzdan?

MOREBRED: Our good Sheriff has suffered with us. Unfortunately his bad back will not permit him to put an end to Snarzdan.

FIRST PEASANT: Well, something had better be done darned soon, Lord Morebred, or we're going to pack it all up and move off to some safer harbor.

SECOND PEASANT: To be sure, living closer to the Vikings, Franks and Beans would be less dangerous than hanging around here.

MOREBRED: My poor, poor peasants. I hear your pleas. Go. Till the fields and harvest the crops that have not yet been destroyed. I swear I'll solve our dragon dilemma posthaste. Go. Go in peace.

SOUND EFFECTS: *The sound of footsteps.*

MOREBRED: *(Continuing)* Are they all gone, Morrie?

MORRIE: Yes, your highness.

MOREBRED: Geez! What a bunch of big babies! Where the heck is that lazy sheriff? He is supposed to keep this riffraff away from my castle walls. *(Calling)* Rottingwood!

ROTTINGWOOD: *(From a distance)* Yes, Lord Morebred? I'm up here in the castle keep.

MOREBRED: Put down that bag of doughnuts and get over here, you fool.

ROTTINGWOOD: *(Still from a distance)* Right away, your grace.

MOREBRED: What were you doing in the keep?

ROTTINGWOOD: Well, your highness, I was counting the sheep and I fell asleep.

MORRIE: You keep the sheep in the keep?

MOREBRED: Of course! We don't want Snarzdan to roast our sheep and wipe out our wool supply. Who's watching the sheep now?

ROTTINGWOOD: Lady Bo Peep, your grace.

MOREBRED: Bo Peep? I hope she doesn't take them for a walk again. *(To Sheriff Rottingwood)* Listen, Rottingwood, the peasants are revolting.

ROTTINGWOOD: Boy, don't I know it! Some of them haven't bathed in years.

MOREBRED: No, I don't mean that way. They're threatening to leave the manor.

ROTTINGWOOD: Oh, that's bad. We're broke already. And if the peasants don't pay their taxes, we will be in the poorhouse.

MOREBRED: If I could only hire a mercenary army to slay that serpent Snarzdan. But alas, with the crops all roasted to a crisp during this past month, there is not a coin in our castle coffer.

Morrie: I fear even the most valiant warrior would be no match for the wicked Snarzdan, Lord Morebred. Dragons have only one thing that cures their madness.

Morebred: And what would that be, Morrie?

Morrie: The death of a damsel. We must seek out a darling dainty damsel for the dragon to devour. Once he has devoured her, he will depart.

Morebred: How do you know this, Morrie? You're a wizard, not a dragonologist.

Morrie: I read it in the *Dragon's Digest Quarterly*. I also read that she must be gentle in spirit, kind of heart . . .

Rottingwood: And soft in head! Do you think we could ever find someone in our manor dense enough to agree to be our sacrifice for the dragon? And "dense" isn't the only problem. Have you seen the local damsels lately? I would not describe them as dainty, your highness. They work hard in our fields. They are strong, not dainty.

Morebred: Good point, Rottingwood. There are no damsels in our dell that would fit the bill of being dainty. We need to commence a *quest* for one.

Sound Effect: *Knock at door.*

Morrie: Hark! Who could be knocking upon our drawbridge door?

Sound Effect: *Door opening.*

Sara Lee: Bonjour, monsieurs. And how are you today?

Rottingwood: Getting better all the time. It's a dainty damsel!

Sara Lee: My name is Sara Lee Antoinette. Would you care to purchase some of my wares?

Morebred: I am Lord Morebred, high mayor of this manor. This is my advisor and personal secretary, Morrie.

Morrie: Howdy.

Sara Lee: Bonjour.

Morebred: And this is the high constable of Toadfat, Sheriff Rottingwood.

Rottingwood: The pleasure is mine, my fair lady.

Sara Lee: *(With an exaggerated French accent)* Ooolala! I love zee man in uniform.

Morebred: What are you selling, Miss Antoinette?

Sara Lee: I have zee most delicious line of snack cakes ever created, Lord Morbid.

Morebred: That is Morebred. Lord Morebred, not Morbid.

Sara Lee: Oh, excuse-zay-mwa. I travel over hill and dale selling my unique bakery creations, gentlemen. My breads are zee toast of France. Would you care to barter for some of them? Yes? No? Maybe zo?

Morebred: Oh sure. But I fear we have very little gold. Sheriff Rottingwood, why don't you get the fine jewelry which we can trade for Miss Antoinette's wares?

Rottingwood: You mean the silver bracelets?

Morebred: Right!

Sara Lee: I just love zee jewelry.

Sound Effect: *Sound of rattling chains*

Sara Lee: *(Continuing)* Oh, my. This is rather unusual jewelry. Heavy, too. Lord Morbid, are you sure these are zee jewels of your castle? They don't fit well.

Morebred: That is Lord Morebred, my dear, and these jewels shall fit our purpose just fine. Hahahahaha!

Sound Effect: *A scream*

Narrator #1: Bound in shackles, the dainty damsel Sara Lee is led away in distress to the dreaded dragon's lair.

Narrator #2: It is located down in the Grizzlyham Grotto by Lake Lancelot.

Narrator #3: Poor Sara Lee's fate seems to be in the dragon's jaws.

Sara Lee: *(Weeping)* Oh, please, spare my life, monsieurs. I promise you a lifetime supply of my cakes — at discount prices, of course. Morrie, you look like such an honest man. How can you allow them to do this to me?

Morrie: My child, this is the only way to save our manor. Think what a noble cause your sacrifice will serve. Ballads will be written in your honor.

Sara Lee: But what if I give the dragon indigestion? High cholesterol runs in my family tree.

Morebred: Ah, saturated fat may ground Snarzdan for good.

Sara Lee: *(Crying)* Oh, woe is me!

Rottingwood: Lord Morebred, look! A stranger approaches.

Sound Effect: *Casual whistling*

Rottingwood: *(Continuing, as he sees Clem Squiggly enter)* Halt, stranger! Pray, who are you?

Clem: Me? Why, I am Clem Squiggly, simple squab and squash farmer and squid salesman from Squirrel Square.

Morrie: Ah, a journeyman.

Clem: I suppose so.

Morebred: Well, then I suggest that you just keep journeying on, my fine fellow. My name is Lord Morebred, high mayor of Toadfat Manor.

Sara Lee: Please, please, kind sir. You must save me from these men.

Clem: Whatever is wrong, fair maiden?

Sara Lee: The wicked Lord Morebred and his evil wizard are going to throw me to the dreaded dragon Snarzdan, just to save their miserable little manor.

Morebred: This has nothing to do with you, squid boy.

Clem: Well, maybe it does have nothing to do with me, and then again maybe it does. I think you're being just a tad rude about this whole thing, Lord Morbid.

Morebred: That's Morebred! Morebred! Can't you simple-minded fools get it right? Sheriff Rottingwood, draw your sword and skewer this squid salesman.

Sound Effect: *Sound of sword being drawn.*

Rottingwood: Do you want to taste my blade, squash farmer?

Clem: Not particularly. Listen can't we all just talk this thing out? I mean does this poor lady have to be sacrificed to save your manor?

Morebred: Yes!

Morrie: Well, not exactly.

Morebred: Morrie, what do you mean?

Morrie: There was a footnote in that article in the *Dragon's Digest Quarterly*: If a true champion can vanquish the dragon in the name of a darling dainty damsel's honor, then the damsel does not need to be devoured. Do you get my meaning, your grace?

Morebred: Oh, I see.

Sara Lee: Oh, kind sir, are you a true champion?

Clem: Well, I don't like to brag, but I am the Squab and Squash Eating Champion of Squirrel Square.

Morebred: Close enough!

Rottingwood: Your grace! This is suicide.

Morebred: Well, let's hope so. We can kill two birds with one stone, so to speak.

Rottingwood: Couldn't we just send the lad to Knight School for a day or so?

There's No Ages Like Dark Ages . . .

Morebred: There is no time, my good sheriff.

Clem: Besides, I'm an early riser. I don't stay up too late.

Rottingwood: Could we at least make him a Knight of the Square Table, Lord Morebred?

Morebred: A splendid suggestion, Sheriff Rottingwood. Come, my fine farmer. Kneel before me and become a Knight of the Toadfat Square Table.

Sara Lee: Oh, goody, goody, goody!

Morebred: Rottingwood, draw the noble sword Exapplecore from its scabbard, so that I may dub this lad a knight. Morrie, recite the Toadfat Oath of Chivalry.

Morrie: Clem Squiggly, in the name of chivalry, do you swear to defend the realm of Toadfat with every drop of your life's blood?

Clem: Oh, you betcha!

Morrie: And do you swear to defend the honor of the fair Sara Lee Antoinette in the challenge of mortal combat?

Clem: Uh, could we leave out the word "mortal?"

Morrie: Sorry, it is part of the text.

Clem: All righty then. I do!

Morebred: Then by the power vested in me as high lord and mayor of the burg of Toadfat, I hereby dub thee Sir Clem Squiggly!

Sara Lee: Oh, my hero!

Morrie: Let us move swiftly before Snarzdan strikes again.

Narrator #1: So the courageous Clem sallies forth to do battle with the wicked worm of a dragon and defend the dainty damsel, Sara Lee Antoinette's honor.

Narrator #2: With the greatest amount of stealth, the bold band approaches Grizzlyham Grotto.

Sound Effect: *Sound of dragon's roar*

Morebred: There is the dragon's den, Sir Clem. Go knock her dead!

Sara Lee: Wait, Sir Clem. Take this silken scarf to serve as your standard as you sally forth into mortal combat.

Clem: Do we have to keep using the word "mortal?" Oh, this scarf is lovely! Do you have anything in blue? This yellow clashes with my tunic.

Rottingwood: My son, here take my chain mail.

Time Warped • Copyright © 2001 • Cottonwood Press, Inc. • 800-864-4297 • www.cottonwoodpress.com

Clem: No, thank you, Sheriff. The truth is I never did learn to read.

Rottingwood: No. The chain mail is my armor.

Sound Effect: *Dragon roar.*

Clem: Whoa! What a horrific howl!

Morrie: Shhh! The dragon approaches!

Snarzdan: Puff, you get back here right this instant! Put down that sheep, you naughty dragon. How many times do I have to tell you: DON'T PLAY WITH YOUR FOOD.

Puff: Oh, Mommy, it's so cute though. Can't I just brush it for a while?

Morebred: (*Whispering*) That's my sheep! Rottingwood, why did you leave Lady Bo Peep to watch the sheep?

Snarzdan: I told you, Puff, put that sheep down! You'll spoil your dinner, young lady.

Puff: What are we having for supper tonight, Momma?

Snarzdan: Peasant under glass, my darling.

Puff: Oh, no, not again. We always have peasant under glass.

Snarzdan: You will have your peasant and like it, Puff. Just be glad you're not like the Ziegfried dragons up north. All they have is diseased rats left over from the Black Death. And that gives them a terrible acid condition. Now come eat your . . . (*Sniffing*) Wait! I smell something. Quick, Puff, get into the cave. I smell you, Englishman. And what is that sweet fragrance as well. French pastry? Come out, come out wherever you are!

Clem: Foul dragon, prepare to meet your death!

Rottingwood: Sir Clem, wait! Take the magical sword Exapplecore with you.

Clem: Thank you, kind Sheriff. Avast! On guard! BEWARE!!!

Snarzdan: Whoa! Stop right there! You really stink, buddy! What is that foul odor? Is that squid? I hate squid. I think I'll just roast you from a distance.

Clem: Oh, yeah, well, we'll just see about that, you sick slimy serpent!

Sound Effect: *Roar and blast of flames.*

Morrie: I can't believe it! Snarzdan just melted the magical sword Exapplecore!

Clem: (*To Snarzdan*) Hey, listen, I hope I wasn't out of line with that slimy serpent crack?

Sound Effect: *Roar*

Clem: (*Continuing*) Wait! Just wait a minute! Hold your flame, my hapless heartburn sufferer. Maybe we can work something out here. You know a cave like this is no proper abode to call your home.

SNARZDAN: It's not?

CLEM: Of course not! Mrs. Snarzdan . . . May I call you Snarzy?

SNARZDAN: Uhhh —

CLEM: O.K., Snarzy, the name is Squiggly. Sir Clem Squiggly. I just happen to be a part-time sales representative of Century Eleven Hundred Realty. And I think I can work a deal with you right here. Why, I can free you from this drab, dingy, shabby, musty port-hole of an existence and put you smack dab in the garden spot of all England.

SNARZDAN: Garden spot?

CLEM: That's right, Snarzy, I'm talking garden spot — primo property to be sure. Here, walk with me; talk with me. How does a condo on the coast grab you? Floor to ceiling wall-hangings, wall to wall marble floor, indoor plumbing, stone hearths. Hey, you want pilot lights, you got 'em! Snarzy, we can plop you down smack dab in the middle of rolling lush landscape, bubbly babbling brooks and gorgeous green gardens like Babylon never saw.

SNARZDAN: I do like flowers . . .

CLEM: And flowers you shall have, my dear. Natural spring waters will make those silver bells and cockleshells grow so well, why you'll be the envy of the entire North Shore. And security, Snarzy, we are talking top security for you and your daughter. You'll be as safe as a bug in a rug. Guard dogs — great Danes, mind you — six-foot walls, and a moat, Snarzy, a mighty moat!

SNARZDAN: A moat?

CLEM: A moat! Sixteen foot deep with hungry crocodiles. Hey, who knows? Maybe it'll be a family reunion, huh? I'll tell you what: you sign now, and we'll throw in a free boat.

SNARZDAN: A free *moata* boat?

CLEM: You got it, Snarzy.

SNARZDAN: Well, I don't know. I've got my daughter Puff to think of, too.

CLEM: Hey, did I mention the schools in the area? We're talking top drawer, college prep caliber. Your little Puff ball will crash the glass ceiling of opportunity.

SNARZDAN: Okay! We'll take it! When do we move?

CLEM: Not to worry your slippery scales over that one, Snarzy. King Arthur's Vanguard Movers will take care of the whole ball of wax.

SNARZDAN: Thank you, Sir Clem. I just wish all knights were as nice as you. Come, Puff. Let us soar to the North Shore.

Sara Lee: Oh, Clem, my hero. You did it! You saved me and all the land.

Clem: Aw shucks, twern't nothing!

Morebred: Magnificent, Sir Clem. I take back all those rotten thoughts I had about you. You shall be my new vassal.

Morrie: But how are we ever going to build that dragon's estate? Our castle coffer is bare.

Clem: Hey, no sweat. Take a gander at all that gold in Snarzdan's grotto.

Rottingham: He is right, Lord Morebred. There is enough gold in there to build a thousand estates. Well done, Sir Clem. Well done!

Morebred: Sir Clem, you are a "true champion." Is there anything I can do for you?

Clem: Would you allow Miss Sara Lee and me to settle down on your manor?

Sara Lee: (*Shyly*) Oh, Sir Clem.

Clem: That is, if she'll marry me?

Sara Lee: Nothing would give me greater pleasure than to become Sara Lee Squiggly!

Morebred: You both shall have the finest fief (*feef*) I have.

Clem: Fief? Maybe a blender would be better . . .

Morebred: Land, Clem. A fief is land — inheritable land. You can farm if you want!

Clem: To tell you the truth, there's something I'd rather do. I've always wanted to sell camels here in England.

Morebred: Very well then. Sir Clem Squiggly will own England's first Camel-lot!

Peasants: Hurray!

Narrator #1:
Legends come and legends go
and some were lost dark ages ago.

Narrator #2:
But as long as tales are told of old,
Clem Squiggly's story will be as good as gold.

THE END

TEACHIER INSTRUCTIONS

WHAT'S THE REAL STORY?

It is important that students understand that *There's No Ages Like Dark Ages* twists facts and fantasy. Some of the terms and names mentioned in *There's No Ages Like Dark Ages* refer to real people, places and things. Others are similar to characters and events from the stories of King Arthur and the Knights of the Round Table.

Have students find out the *real* story behind the items listed on page 87. Depending upon your students and your classroom situation, try one of the following approaches:

Have students individually research the various items, or a selection of the items.
- Divide the items up between different groups of students, and have them report their findings back to the class.
- Make it a contest. See how much of the "real" story students can uncover in one class period, using the Internet, encyclopedias, and other sources.

For your convenience, here is some basic information about each item:

KING ARTHUR. Legendary British hero, said to have been king of the Britons in the 6th century A.D.

QUEEN GUINEVERE. In Arthurian legend, King Arthur's wife, who was also in love with Lancelot.

MORGAN LE FAY. The sorceress sister and enemy of King Arthur.

AVALON. According to Celtic mythology, this island paradise in the western seas is where King Arthur and other heroes went after death.

EXCALIBUR. The name of King Arthur's sword, given to him by the Lady of the Lake.

SOURCES ON THE ARTHURIAN LEGENDS

Young Adult Novels:
The Sword and the Circle: King Arthur and the Knights of the Round Table, by Rosemary Sutcliff
King Arthur and His Knights of the Round Table, by Richard L. Green
The Squire, His Knight, and His Lady, by Gerald Morris
The Light beyond the Forest: The Quest for the Holy Grail, by Rosemary Sutcliff
Quest for a King: Searching for the Real King Arthur, by Catherine M. Andronik
Winter of Magic's Return, by Pamela F. Service
Tomorrow's Magic, by Pamela F. Service
The Last Pendragon, by Robert Rice

Movie and video resources:
The Sword in the Stone
Camelot

Literary sources:
The Mists of Avalon, by Marion Zimmer Bradley
Idylls of the King, by Alfred Lord Tennyson
Le Morte D'Arthur, by Thomas Malory
La Belle Dame Sans Merci, by John Keats

Web sources:
- www.britannia.com/history/h12.html
- www.mythsearch.com/arthur.html
- historymedren.about.com/homework/historymedren/cs/kingarthur/
- www.legends.dm.net/kingarthur/index.html

Time Warped • Copyright © 2001 • Cottonwood Press, Inc. • 800-864-4297 • www.cottonwoodpress.com

MERLIN. A magician and prophet who used magic to help King Arthur.

LANCELOT. The most famous knight of the Round Table. He had a love affair with Queen Guinevere.

GAWAIN. One of King Arthur's knights of the Round Table. His character varies, depending on the story.

GALAHAD. Lancelot's son and the purest of the knights of the Round Table. He alone succeeded in the quest for the Holy Grail.

MORDRED. King Arthur's wicked nephew.

PENDRAGON. A king of Britain and King Arthur's father.

STUDENT INSTRUCTIONS

WHAT'S THE REAL STORY?

Many things in today's world are based on the very old legends of King Arthur. Las Vegas is home to an entire hotel/casino built and designed around the Arthurian legends. The hotel is named Excalibur after King Arthur's magical and powerful sword. Indiana Jones searches for the Holy Grail, another element from the stories of King Arthur, in the movie *Indiana Jones and the Last Crusade.* Toyota even calls one of its popular cars Avalon, which was where Arthur fled after his final battle.

Many items in *There's No Ages Like Dark Ages* are also based on elements from the legends of King Arthur. Look up the names, places and terms below — some which are satirized in this play — to learn more about the real Arthurian legends. Write a short explanation of each term.

KING ARTHUR

QUEEN GUINEVERE

MORGAN LE FAY

AVALON

EXCALIBUR

MERLIN

LANCELOT

GAWAIN

GALAHAD

MORDRED

PENDRAGON

Time Warped • Copyright © 2001 • Cottonwood Press, Inc. • 800-864-4297 • www.cottonwoodpress.com

For Your Information

Feudalism was an economic system of land and taxes that began as a military system. It is associated with the middle ages, a period of European history from roughly 500-1500. Much in literature and movies has glamorized the era of feudalism with its castles and noblemen. In reality, however, it wasn't glamorous at all. It was an accepted form of slavery.

Pyramid: Kings / Nobility: Barons, Lords and Vassals / Knights / Serfs and Peasants

Feudalism was based on a harsh hierarchy. Look at the pyramid above to see how the different levels of society stacked up.

KINGS, at the top of the feudal pyramid, owned vast amounts of lands. The king was believed to have the divine right to his land. In other words, people believed that God had granted him his land and power. This divine right was passed on from father to son.

Feudalism existed almost 1000 years ago, so it was a time when it took many days to travel across even the smallest kingdom. To help rule his great lands, kings "hired" barons.

BARONS were given large lots of land, known as **fiefs or manors**, from the king's kingdom. In return for this land, barons helped the king to maintain control over his large empire. Barons were also required to pay **homage and fealty** to the king. In other words, they had to pay taxes whenever the king asked and provide military protection for the king's land. They also had to govern the land and give their loyal support to the king at all times. When a baron was granted or inherited a fief, he became a **vassal** to the king. The baron was also considered to be **lord** of his manor.

Sometimes barons ran into the same problem as the king, with land that was too large for them to easily manage. When this was the case, a baron would "hire" lords to help him rule his land. Just like the king, he would give a parcel of his land in exchange for homage and fealty. He usually gave his land to a trusted knight or relative.

Lordships were passed down from generation to generation. This created a solid class of nobility that believed it was far superior to the common class of serfs and peasants.

KNIGHTS were the soldiers of the feudal army. Their job was to protect the lord of the manor and his land, and indirectly, protect the king and his power.

SERFS AND PEASANTS made up almost 90 percent of the population in the middle ages. That is why they are at the base of the pyramid. Serfs and peasants worked harder and gained less than anyone else in feudal society. They were required to work the land of the lord and often pay taxes to the manor as well. Worse, noblemen were often cruel to the working peasants because they believed that they were far superior to them.

Serfs and peasants were very much like slaves. Lords often forced the peasants to use and pay for services provided by the manor. A lord had the right to grant marriages and charge and collect taxes whenever he wished. He also held absolute power in handing out punishment.

Serfs were bound to the land they worked. If a lord sold or gave away his land, the serfs were sold along with it. Peasants often died from overwork, starvation and exploitation.

Oddly enough, serfs and peasants often wished to live under a lord. They believed that the lord protected them from barbarians and invading armies. They felt safer working near the walls of a castle than in unprotected territory.

THE ROMAN CATHOLIC CHURCH also held great power in the system of feudalism. Clergymen were often equal in power to the lords. At times, the church was even more powerful than any king because the church owned and managed land all over Europe. With feudalism, land equaled power.

The church did not seek taxes from peasants and serfs, but it did acquire a lot of money from medieval peasants. Peasants believed that the harder they worked and the more money they gave to the church, the better the afterlife would be for them. The beliefs of the peasants worked greatly in the favor of both the church and the lord of the manor.

PRIMOGENITURE was a custom of the middle ages whereby land was passed down to only the eldest son. People preferred to pass on land to only one heir because they didn't want their land to become greatly divided. If it was divided, every generation would receive a smaller and smaller parcel of land. Remember: During feudal times, more land meant more power.

While primogeniture made sense for maintaining the integrity of the land, it created other problems. The biggest problem was what happened to the other children of a lord. The female children were married off to other landowners. This was a great way to join two fiefdoms in political loyalty. It was also a way for a lord to increase his political power.

Some of the lord's other sons would continue to work on the manor under their older brother. Often times, the second son was expected to join the church. This insured that the manor had allies within the church, which would, of course, bring the fiefdom even more power. Finally, some sons began leaving the countryside for more urban areas, which eventually led way to the industrial revolution and the end of feudalism.

Coat of Arms

The coat of arms dates all the way back to the 12th century. Just as sports teams and schools today have special mascots and colors, the coat of arms in the middle ages helped to identify who was who during a battle. Later on, the coat of arms also became a way to show family ties and genealogy, alliances, property ownership and profession.

A coat of arms almost always contains a shield, which becomes the center. Symbolic colors, animals and other objects are added on or around the shield to represent whatever the knight, family or organization wants to emphasize. The symbols used in a coat of arms are called charges. Below is a list of colors and charges commonly used in designing a coat of arms:

COLORS

Yellow or gold: Generosity
White or silver: Peace and sincerity
Black: Constancy, sometimes grief
Blue: Loyalty and truth
Red: Military fortitude and magnanimity
Green: Hope, joy and sometimes loyalty in love
Purple: Royal majesty, sovereignty and justice
Tan: Worthy ambition

COMMON CHARGES

Lion: Courage
Tiger: Great fierceness and valor
Bear: Ferocity in the protection of family
Wolf: Endurance and victory
Elephant: Courage and strength
Panther: Beautiful woman who is very tender and loving to her children but will fiercely defend them
Horse: Always willing to do what is asked
Bull or Ox: Brave and kind
Goat: Brains over brawn
Lamb: Gentleness and patience
Fox: Wit, wisdom and good judgement
Dog: Courage and loyalty
Cat: Alertness, courage and prophecy
Bee: Hard-working
Ant and Spider: Hard-working, wisdom and fortune
Grasshopper: Wisdom and nobility
Eagle: Action, speed and ingenuity
Falcon or Hawk: Eagerness
Owl: Wisdom, alertness and wit
Peacock: Beauty and pride
Swan: A lover of poetry and harmony
Dove: Peace
Tortoise: Invulnerable
Unicorn: Extreme courage
Dragon: The bravest defender of treasures
Pegasus: Extreme smarts and brain power
Mermaid: Eloquence
Buck and Deer: Peace and Harmony.
Heart: Charity and sincerity
Hand: Faith, sincerity and justice
Arm: Hard-working
Leg, Shoe and Foot: Strength, stability and one who travels
Pen: Educated and good at writing
Snake: Wisdom
Sun: Glory and splendor
Moon: Serene power
Fire: Zeal
Lightning: Forceful and clear
Horse Shoe: Good luck
Trunk of a Tree: Reverent and respectful
Wheel: Fortune

Time Warped • Copyright © 2001 • Cottonwood Press, Inc. • 800-864-4297 • www.cottonwoodpress.com

Design Your Own Coat of Arms

Use the space below or your own paper to design your own personal coat of arms. Remember that everything you include on your coat of arms should have a symbolic reason for being there. Look at the lists of colors and charges on the previous page to get ideas for your design. You can also include your own symbols on your coat of arms.

Once you are done designing your coat of arms, write an explanation for every object and color you have included.

If you are interested in looking at existing coats of arms or want further information, please visit this web site: www.designsofwonder.com.

ALLITERATION

"We must seek out a darling dainty damsel to serve as the dragon's delight. Once the dreaded dragon has devoured the damsel, he will depart."

The lines above, from *There's No Ages Like Dark Ages*, may cause you to wonder, "What's up with all the *d's?* The answer is *alliteration*. Alliteration refers to the repetition of similar consonant sounds in a short section of writing. Alliteration emphasizes the words with similar sounds and helps link the ideas that the words express. It can also be used for a humorous effect, as in the lines above from the play.

Try your hand at writing alliteration. Write five alliterative sentences based on topics from the box below. Use a different alliterative sound for each sentence.

> school lunch • Coca-Cola • lizards • volleyball • dancing • outer space
> calico cats • soccer • pizza • frisbee • Halloween • veggies • tubas
> flamingos • Backstreet Boys • Spaghetti O's • moose • toenails • fungus
> New York Yankees • purple • squirrels • computer • french fries
> tie-dye • hamster • Fourth of July • accordions • chat rooms

1.

2.

3.

4.

5.

RENAISSANCE REFORM SCHOOL

Renaissance Reform School

CHARACTERS

EARNEST P. POTHOLE. Co-host of the radio program, "Highways to History."
FRANKLIN C. DETOUR. Co-host of "Highways to History."
MICHELANGELO BOYARDEE. An artist of little talent.
DONNAJELLO MANICOTTI. Another artist of little talent.
LEONARDO DA LINGUINI. Still another artist of little talent.
LORETTA DE MEDICI *(MED-uh-chee)*. The sister of the great patron of the arts, Lorenzo de Medici.
MADAME ISABELLA D'LATTE. (duh-LA-tay) A private tutor in the Renaissance arts.
MISS CANOLI. Loretta de Medici's assistant.
PRINCE JULIUS PORTABELLY OF PROVOLONE. The prince of Italy.
BENNY BARTHOLOMEW. Prince Julius' advisor.
SOUND EFFECTS. This "role" can be performed by a group of people. If the play is recorded as a radio show or performed in front of a group, the sound effects can be prepared carefully ahead of time. If the play is read aloud in class, quick and easy methods of simulating sound effects should be improvised as the play is read. For example, the sound effects group might hum when music is specified, or drop books on a desk top when crashing noises are indicated.

SETTING: A present day radio program.

FRANK: Good day, everyone. I'm Frank . . .

EARNEST: And I'm Earnest.

FRANK: Welcome to another episode of *Highways to History*. We are your travel guides, Professor Franklin C. Detour . . .

EARNEST: . . . and Professor Earnest P. Pothole. Today we are journeying to another fascinating time and place: the Renaissance!

Renaissance Reform School

SOUND EFFECTS. *Trumpets blare.*

FRANK: The Renaissance is known as an era of rebirth. The Renaissance period rescued a dismal Europe from the depths of the Dark Ages by reviving the cultural, social, political and artistic values of ancient Greece and Rome.

EARNEST: Nicely phrased, Frank.

FRANK: Thank you.

EARNEST: During the Renaissance, ideas that had been lost or suppressed were rediscovered . . .

FRANK: . . . and became respected again!

EARNEST: Quite true! Quite true! It was a time when art flourished. Powerful and wealthy merchants became patrons for scholars, inventors and artists.

FRANK: Yes, wealthy patrons helped to pay the cost for building churches and palaces, and they paid artists to decorate these buildings with their artwork. Some patrons even went so far as to provide protection and housing for artists, so they could create their works of art without worrying how they were going to support themselves.

EARNEST: The most well-known of the patrons was Lorenzo de Medici *(MED-uh-chee)*, the wealthy banker of the Italian city-state of Florence. He was considered by many to be an incompetent banker and a tyrannical leader, but he is best known and loved for his contributions to the arts. He helped to mold such artists as Sandro Botticelli and Michelangelo.

FRANK: But few know about another patron, de Medici's twin sister, Loretta.

EARNEST: Quite correct, Franklin. Between Lorenzo and Loretta raged one of the most intense rivalries in the history of the art world. We would know nothing at all about her, had it not been for their greatest confrontation of all, which we are going to tell you about today.

FRANK: In an effort to compete with her brother's famous court, Loretta de Medici held interviews with artists, trying to find special and talented people like those sponsored by her brother. She wanted to be known as a great patron of the arts herself.

EARNEST: But only a lucky few artists would gain acceptance to her court. Let's go back in history and listen in . . .

GOING BACK IN TIME . . .

LORETTA: Miss Canoli, has the talent agency sent over any applicants for my court? Prince Julius Portabelly of Provolone's Art Exhibition is only a month away.

CANOLI: Yes, Lady de Medici. I contacted them, and they said they have sent over the cream of the crop. In fact, the applicants have arrived.

LORETTA: Wonderful! Send in the first artist.

SOUND EFFECTS: *Sound of a chair sliding.*

LEONARDO: *(Entering)* Hi! How are you? Here's my resume.

SOUND EFFECTS: *Sound of paper rustling.*

LORETTA: You are Leonardo da Linguini?

LEONARDO: That's my name.

LORETTA: I see here that you consider yourself a true Renaissance man. What talents do you have that would be an asset to my court?

LEONARDO: Well, I paint a lot. Here. Here is a sample of my work.

LORETTA: My goodness. The woman in this painting looks like she is in pain!

LEONARDO: That's why I call this the *Moaning Lisa*.

LORETTA: My brother has a painter named Leonardo da Vinci who did a painting called the *Mona Lisa*.

LEONARDO: That guy stinks as an artist! His painting is so boring compared to mine! Who do you think people are going to remember hundreds of years from now, me or him?

LORETTA: Uh, I don't know. What else can you do?

LEONARDO: Lots of stuff. I play the spoons.

SOUND EFFECTS: *Sound of spoons playing*

LEONARDO: *(Continuing)* Not bad, huh? Oh, and I can juggle cantaloupes.

SOUND EFFECTS: *Rhythmic sound of hands catching objects.*

LORETTA: Oh, do be careful. Those cantaloupes are for tonight's banquet. I don't want them . . .

SOUND EFFECTS: *Sound of cantaloupes hitting the ground*

LORETTA: . . . bruised.

LEONARDO: Oops. Sorry about that. Just cut the bruised spots off. Nobody will know. Oh yes. I can also sing "Lady of Spain, I Adore You" with a mouthful of walnuts.

LORETTA: I'd rather you not sing, please.

LEONARDO: *(Spoken through mouthful of walnuts)* Well, you're the boss. *(Removing walnuts)* I hope.

LORETTA: Any other, uh, talents?

LEONARDO: Certainly! I can stand on my head for about forty-three minutes before I pass out. Let me show you.

LORETTA: That's all right. I'll take your word for it. *(Aside, to Miss Canoli)* Miss Canoli, do we have a lot of applicants?

CANOLI: Only two more.

LORETTA: *(Sighing and turning to Leonardo)* I guess we'll let you into the court, Mr. da Linguini.

LEONARDO: Hey, thanks, lady! You won't be sorry.

SOUND EFFECTS: *Sound of chair sliding as Leonardo exits.*

LORETTA: Miss Canoli, who's next?

CANOLI: There is a gentleman named Michelangelo waiting.

LORETTA: *(Excitedly)* Oh, Michelangelo Bounarroti? *(Bwo-nar-RO-tee)* I've heard of him ... He's a *great* artist!

CANOLI: No, not that guy. The one waiting is Michelangelo Boyardee.

LORETTA: *(Disappointed)* Oh. Very well. Send in Mr. Boyardee.

SOUND EFFECTS: *Sound of footsteps as Michelangelo enters.*

MICHELANGELO: Yo! What's up?

LORETTA: Good day Mr. Boyardee.

MICHELANGELO: Can I get a plate of Beefaroni or something? I'm starving here.

LORETTA: Let's review your credits first. So, Mr. Boyardee ...

MICHELANGELO: Hey, call me Mickey B.

LORETTA: All right, Mickey B., do you do any painting or sculpting?

MICHELANGELO: Yessiree! I'm really into painting ceilings.

LORETTA: Ceilings? Interesting! Do you paint the ceilings of churches or chapels?

MICHELANGELO: No. Mostly I paint the ceilings of garages and sheds and places like that. Here are some sketches of some of my jobs.

LORETTA: I see. Well, do you have any other skills to bring to my court, Mickey B.?

MICHELANGELO: Here! Check out this sculpture.

LORETTA: It's a pyramid.

MICHELANGELO: That's right! Hey, you're good. It's a pyramid made completely out of salt tablets. And how about this one?

Loretta: Another pyramid?

Michelangelo: Yes. And this one is made totally out of sugar cubes. Want a lick?

Loretta: No, I'll pass.

Michelangelo: And take a gander at this one.

Loretta: A pyramid again?

Michelangelo: You got it! And this one's made out of chocolate candy bars.

Loretta: Do you sculpt anything but pyramids?

Michelangelo: What? You don't like pyramids?

Loretta: Pyramids are wonderful. *(To Miss Canoli)* Have we got any more applicants waiting?

Canoli: Just one.

Loretta: *(Sighing and turning to Michelangelo)* Welcome to my court, Mickey B. Miss Canoli, get him a plate of Beefaroni. And a big napkin.

Michelangelo: Thanks a million, Lady Medici. You won't regret this!

Loretta: That remains to be seen. Send in the next applicant, Miss Canoli.

Miss Canoli: Our next artist is Sir Donajello Manicotti.

Sound effects: *Crashing sound of tripping over a chair as Donajello enters.*

Loretta: Welcome, Mr. Manicotti.

Donajello: Call me by my first name: Donajello.

Loretta: Very well, Donajello. What is your story? What do you have to offer my court?

Donajello: I am the finest acrobat and tumbler in all of Venice. My brother Dominic and I once performed for the Pope.

Loretta: Impressive!

Donajello: Would you like to see a flip?

Loretta: Well, uh, I —

Donajello: High Up!!! *(He leaps into the air to do a back flip.)*

Loretta: Hey, watch it!

Sound effects: *Sound of crashing as he falls*

Loretta: *(Continuing)* You broke my table!

Renaissance Reform School

Donajello: Oops! Sorry about that.

Loretta: Do you usually run into things and break them when you perform your acrobatic stunts?

Donajello: *(Timidly)* Occasionally.

Loretta: Where's your brother?

Donajello: He should be getting out of the hospital in the next few weeks.

Loretta: I see. *(She turns in desperation to Miss Canoli.)* Hasn't *anyone* else shown up?

Miss Canoli: No. That's the last artist.

Loretta: *(To Donajello)* All right, Donajello, we'll work with you.

Donajello: Oh, Miss Medici, you make me jump for joy!

Loretta: Save it for later, O.K.? Go get some food and meet the other artists. *(To Miss Canoli)* Miss Canoli, are you sure this was the cream of the crop?

Canoli: Yes, my lady. I could go back and get that Gepetto guy and his puppet that you interviewed from yesterday . . .

Loretta: No, we don't need any ventriloquists. We have to whip these guys into shape to get them to compete with my brother's court. Why does he get all the good ones?

Canoli: I don't know, ma'am. Maybe these three will be more presentable after they go to our Renaissance Finishing School.

Loretta: Or maybe we ought to send them to the Renaissance Reform School.

Canoli: Miss Medici. We don't have a reform school.

Loretta: I know, I know. Let's at least get these guys some extra tutoring. Send for Madame Isabella d'Latte. She can tutor them. We'll create our own private reform school. If she can't make silk purses out of these sow's ears, nobody can.

Coming back to the present . . .

Earnest: Essential to all Renaissance courts was training at the Renaissance Finishing School. It was here that artists learned the proper manners of a true Renaissance Man.

Frank: Loretta de Medici's Court, however, needed more help than a finishing school could give. The renowned Madame Isabella d'Latte was known far and wide as a demanding — and excellent — tutor.

Going back in time . . .

Isabella: For goodness sakes, sit up straight you three! And get your finger out your ear, Michelangelo.

SOUND EFFECTS: *Sound of popping.*

DONAJELLO: How did you get that get stuck in your ear, anyway, Michelangelo?

MICHELANGELO: Call me Mickey B.

ISABELLA: No! In Miss Loretta's Court you are Michelangelo. Address one another properly, or you will find yourself back in the gutter.

SOUND EFFECTS: *Sound of stick hitting desk.*

MICHELANGELO: Ow! Hey, watch your ruler, lady!

ISABELLA: Now who can tell me Rule Number 3 of the Standard Renaissance Manners Handbook?

DONAJELLO: Isn't that the one about not bragging about your great accomplishments and superior intellect?

ISABELLA: No, that is Number 5, and you three don't really have to worry about that one.

LEONARDO: Oh, oh! I know! I know!

ISABELLA: You don't have to wave your arms and stand on your chair, Leonardo. Get down from there and just tell us.

LEONARDO: Do not tell sad stories at parties or at the dinner table.

ISABELLA: Correct.

MICHELANGELO: Show off!

LEONARDO: You're just jealous!

DONAJELLO: Teacher's pet.

ISABELLA: Silence! Silence! *(Aside)* Where's my aspirin root? *(To the artists)* Now since we are on the dinnertime subject, let us recite the Rules of the Table that I taught you at our last session. Rule Number One?

LEONARDO/MICHELANGELO/DONAJELLO: *(Together)* Don't blow your nose into your napkin.

ISABELLA: Yes. Number Two?

LEONARDO/MICHELANGELO/DONAJELLO: Don't offer anyone fruit when you've already taken a bite.

ISABELLA: Correct.

MICHELANGELO: What if it's just a little bite?

ISABELLA: For the twelfth time, Michelangelo, it is never acceptable. Now, Rule Number Three?

Leonardo/Michelangelo/Donajello: Don't sleep on the table during the main course.

Isabella: No, no, no! Not just during the main course. Never sleep on the table during dinner at *any* time. Rule Number Four?

Leonardo/Michelangelo/Donajello: Do not fill both sides of your mouth with so much food that your cheeks stick out like a chipmunk.

Isabella: *(Exasperated sigh)* Correct.

Leonardo: But what if we want to save some for later?

Michelangelo: Just wrap it up into a napkin and shove it in your pocket.

> **Sound Effects:** *Sound of ruler smacking table loudly.*

Isabella: No, no, no! It is not acceptable to save the food for later.

Donajello: I knew that.

Leonardo: Did not!

Donajello: Did, too! Did, too!

> **Sound Effects:** *Sound of chair tumbling over.*

Michelangelo: Boy, what a klutz!

Leonardo: Am not!

Donajello: Are too!

Leonardo: Am not!

Donajello: Are too!

Isabella: Stop it! Stop it! Stop it! Cease this bickering! You three are impossible!

Loretta: *(Entering)* Madame d'Latte, what is wrong?

> **Sound Effects:** *Sound of ruler breaking.*

Isabella: Everything is wrong! These three are hopeless! Why don't you send them over for a practice dinner with that woman Lucretia Borgia?

Michelangelo: Hey, isn't she the one who poisons all her guests?

Isabella: *(In mock surprise)* Oh really? Never mind. Do with them what you want! I quit! These stooges are beyond my help!

> **Sound Effects:** *Sound of door slamming.*

Loretta: Now look what you've done! Madame d'Latte was the finest instructor in all of Italy.

LEONARDO: Oh, I don't think she was very good.

MICHELANGELO: Trust me, we'll be better off without her.

LORETTA: Well, it can't be helped now. Let's talk about the art show. How are you coming with your exhibits? The show is in a matter of weeks, and I do so want my artists to look as good as my brother Lorenzo's. What have you three come up with so far?

DONAJELLO: I've been working on a triple back flip.

LEONARDO: I invented this back scratcher.

MICHELANGELO: I've got a new sculpture finished. It's of a . . .

LORETTA: Another pyramid?

MICHELANGELO: How did you know?

LORETTA: A lucky guess.

MICHELANGELO: This one's made out of chunks of cheddar cheese.

LORETTA: *(Sarcastically)* Wonderful.

CANOLI: *(Entering)* Lady Medici, we just received this letter from Prince Portabelly's head secretary, Benny Bartholomew.

SOUND EFFECTS: *Sound of envelope tearing open.*

LORETTA: *(Scanning the letter)* Oh, no! The Art Exhibition has been moved up to *this* weekend. And, worse, the rules have been changed!

CANOLI: But how can that be? Changed to what?

LORETTA: It has been changed to a food competition. It is called the Portabelly's Pillsdairy Bake-off. I'm doomed! Lorenzo's artists are sure to be artists with food as well. They will embarrass us for sure. *(She exits, weeping.)*

CANOLI: Alas, our lady will never be able to defeat her brother and the rest of the high courts of Italy. I wish you three knew how to do something well.

LEONARDO: If the Portabelly Pillsdairy Bake-off is a cooking contest, we can do that.

CANOLI: You? You three can cook? I didn't think you knew how to do anything.

MICHELANGELO: Well, you were wrong, and Leo's right. We can cook up a storm.

CANOLI: Why didn't you ever tell us?

DONAJELLO: You never asked.

CANOLI: Do you think you three can come up with a winning recipe by Saturday?

MICHELANGELO: It's in the bag!

Leonardo: We'll blow their oven doors off.

Coming back to the present . . .

Earnest: When the day of Prince Portabelly's Pillsdairy Bake-off arrives, all the noblemen and noblewomen of Italy are there, including a rather despondent Loretta de Medici.

Frank: As the dishes are brought to Prince Portabelly's Food Court, the prince samples the recipes with careful consideration. His advisor, Benny Bartholomew, is his guide.

Going back in time . . .

Prince: Good day to you, Lady Loretta. Are you here to support your brother?

Loretta: (*Dejectedly*): I suppose so.

Prince: Come, my dear. Accompany us during the judging. Ah! What have we here, Benny?

Sound Effects: *Sound of soft music and clattering dishes.*

Benny: Your Grace, this is the Grilled Chateaux Cheese Sandwich Deluxe from the court of Lady Beatrice of Venice.

Prince: Quite interesting. A nice buttery taste for the palate. And this one?

Benny: This is entry number 75, The Fluffer-Nutter Surprise from Sir Delmonico's Court of Naples.

Prince: (*Mumbling*): Kind of sticks to the roof of my mouth.

Benny: And here is the Mystery Meatball Medley sponsored by Sir Mordacai of Milan.

Prince: My, that has an unusual taste. Are you sure this really is meat?

Benny: And here is Lorenzo de Medici's entry.

Prince: Ah, have you saved the best for last?

Benny: Franks and Beans Brisket nestled in artichoke hearts.

Prince: *(In a disappointed tone)* How interesting. *(He turns to Loretta's artists.)* And who are these gentlemen representing?

Loretta: *(Groaning)* Oh, no!

Benny: This is our last entry, Your Highness. The final entry is from Lorenzo de Medici's sister.

Prince: Well, this is a surprise.

Loretta: You can say that again.

PRINCE: Well, this is a surprise.

LORETTA: You can say that again.

PRINCE: *(To Donnajello)* Say, don't I know you?

DONNAJELLO: You have a good memory, your Princeship. I once performed some tumbling for you with my brother —

PRINCE: Oh, no! It's the nut from that performance at the Provolone Palace! He took out the first three rows of the audience!

LEONARDO: Rest easy. Today there is but the finest food to flip for you.

DONNAJELLO: Your Grace, Michelangelo Boyardee, Leonardo de Linguini and I have prepared Pasta Primavera Alfredo Supreme. Tumble that around your mouth!

PRINCE: Mmmm! Delicious! And what is this exquisite beverage?

MICHELANGELO: That was my touch! It's a citrus delight, Orange Julius Creamy Dream — in your honor, of course, your majesty.

DONNAJELLO: And to top it off is this jiggly, wiggly, nervous concoction . . .

PRINCE: Oh my! I don't think I could eat another bite.

LEONARDO: Nonsense. Try it! There's always room for Donnajello.

PRINCE: *(Tasting Donnajello's concoction.)* Attention! Attention! We have a winner. With the greatest pleasure I bestow the Prince Portabelly Pillsdairy Bake-off Gold Award to Lady Loretta de Medici and her Pasta Princes!

SOUND EFFECTS: *Sound of cheers.*

LORETTA: *(Shocked)* What? Prince Portabelly, thank you so very much. Hey, Lorenzo! Eat your artichoke hearts out!

COMING BACK TO THE PRESENT . . .

EARNEST: Finally, Loretta de Medici achieved the recognition she had always so desperately sought.

FRANK: Although her brother went on to be recorded as "Lorenzo the Magnificent," patron of the arts, his sister became the Matron of Italy's finest foods, earning her the title of "Queen of Cuisine."

EARNEST: And you better believe it is true, because I'm Earnest —

FRANK: — and I'm Frank!

TOGETHER: Bidding you so long from *Highways to History!*

THE END

TEACHER INSTRUCTIONS

WHAT'S THE REAL STORY?

It is important that students understand that the *Renaissance Reform School* twists both history and mythology. With "What's the Real Story?" on page 107, they are reminded, or learn for the first time, about some of the terms, characters and events.

Have students find out the *real* story behind the items listed below. Depending upon your students and your classroom situation, try one of the following approaches:

- Have students individually research the various items, or a selection of the items.
- Divide the items up between different groups of students, and have them report their findings back to the class.
- Make it a contest. See how much of the "real" story students can uncover in one class period, using the Internet, encyclopedias, and other sources.

For your convenience, here is a quick background for each item:

FLORENTINE SCHOOL. The name of the major art movement that took place in Florence during the Renaissance.

LUCRETIA BORGIA. Member of an influential Spanish-Italian family and legendary for her crimes and wickedness. Actually, she was beautiful and kind, and the stories are unfounded.

PLATONIC ACADEMY. A school founded by Plato near Athens in 387 B.C. Also, in 15th century Florence, it was a group of scholars who discussed Platonic philosophy and were supported by Lorenzo de Medici.

ANGELO POLIZIANO. An Italian poet, humanist and classical scholar who was a friend of Lorenzo de Medici and a member of the Platonic Academy.

MICHELANGELO BUONARROTI. Italian sculptor, painter, architect, and poet of the Renaissance. Considered to be one of the most influential artists in history, he painted the ceiling of the Sistine Chapel.

SANDRO BOTTICELLI. Italian painter known for his portraits of the Medici family and his classical paintings, such as "Birth of Venus" and "Primavera" *(Spring)*.

MEDICI TOMBS. Elaborate tombs designed by Michelangelo for the members of the Medici family. They are located in the Church of San Lorenzo in Florence.

LEONARDO DA VINCI. Famous painter, sculptor, architect and engineer who lived from 1452-1519. He had ideas about science that were way ahead of his time. Two of his famous paintings are the "Mona Lisa" and the "Last Supper."

DONATELLO. A Renaissance artist who lived in Florence. He is sometimes known as the father of modern sculpture. He lived from 1386-1466.

WHAT'S THE REAL STORY?

Lorenzo de Medici, known as. Lorenzo the Magnificent by many Florentines, was a dabbling artist. However, he is best known as being a patron of the arts, probably the most famous patron ever. He provided money for education and housing to artists whose work he liked and admired. This made it possible for artists like Michelangelo, Botticelli and Da Vinci to work on their art without worrying about working at a regular job to earn their wages.

Lorenzo de Medici gathered artists, poets and intellects at his court to fund and nurture their talents. He was also a gifted poet. His poetry was also noteworthy because it was written in the vernacular. This means that he wrote poetry in his local Tuscan dialect, instead of writing in the formal and classic Latin. While this may seem unimportant to us now, it was very extraordinary during Medici's day.

To learn more about Lorenzo de Medici and his time, find out about the items below, using encyclopedias, the Internet or other research tools. Write a short explanation of each item.

FLORENTINE SCHOOL

LUCRETIA BORGIA

PLATONIC ACADEMY

ANGELO POLIZIANO

MICHELANGELO BUONARROTI

SANDRO BOTTICELLI

MEDICI TOMBS

LEONARDO DA VINCI

DONATELLO

Renaissance People

Michelangelo Buoyardee, Leonardo da Linguini, and Donajello bear some resemblance to their real-life inspirations of Michelangelo Buonarroti, Leonardo da Vinci, and Donatello. Use the charts below to compare and contrast the fictional play characters with their real-life counterparts.

<u>MICHELANGELO BOYARDEE</u>   <u>MICHELANGELO BUONARROTI</u>

<u>LEONARDO DA LINGUINI</u>   <u>LEONARDO DA VINCI</u>

<u>DONNAJELLO</u>   <u>DONATELLO</u>

Handbook of Rules

In *Renaissance Reform School,* Isabelle d'Latte quizzes her students on the *Standard Renaissance Rules Handbook.* Some of the rules from the handbook include:

- *Don't blow your nose into your napkin.*
- *Do not fill both sides of your mouth with so much food that your cheeks stick out like a chipmunk.*

See if you can write a humorous rule book for situations in today's world. Pick a specific setting from the list below (or choose one of your own) and write ten humorous rules for your own Standard Modern Day Rules Handbook.

at school	at Grandma's house	in the locker room
at the table	at the mall with friends	on the phone
in the car	at the mall with parents	during detention
on a date	watching television	on the school bus
at a band recital	playing PlayStation	in the cafeteria

STANDARD MODERN DAY RULES HANDBOOK FOR _____

1.

2.

3.

4.

5.

6.

7.

8.

9.

10.

ANSWER KEYS

THE MUMMY'S PURSE

WHAT'S THE REAL STORY?

PAGE 27

See Teacher Instructions, pages 25-26.

IT'S ALL IN THE NAME

PAGE 30

Answers will vary. A sample answer:

Bill Lazemode
Daisy Frill
Willy Goodheart
Bertha Plumpbottom

Muscles Malone — This guy works all day loading heavy boxes into trucks and never complains. He spends every lunch hour at the gym, where he lifts weights. When he's not playing soccer with his "over 30" soccer team after work, he makes extra money delivering refrigerators for an appliance store.

THE IDIODYSSEY

WHAT'S THE REAL STORY?

PAGE 45

See Teacher Instructions, pages 42-44.

TWISTING HISTORY

PAGE 48

Answers will vary. A sample answer:

I think that women are usually not treated the same as men and that men usually make more money than women do. It is better than it used to be for women because now they can go to school to be doctors, engineers, lawyers, dentists and other professions. Still, there are not as many women who go into these professions. More women become nurses, teachers and secretaries.

    Boys and girls are treated pretty much the same in school, except when it comes to sports. Then the boys' teams get all the attention and usually have better uniforms and get to go more places and play in more tournaments. They are also the ones who are elected to the offices in the school, but not always. It seems that boys are always expected to do better after they grow up. They are supposed to make a lot of money and take care of their wives and children.

    Personally, I think the biggest difference in society for men and women is in the government. There has never been a woman president or vice-president. This is the most unfair thing of all because women do not have a say in the most important laws of the country and in decisions that affect their own lives. If this would change, then everything else would probably change and women would have more power to help each other.

I think ironic means that it makes no real sense to treat women differently than men when the society believes in treating all people equally, which is what a true democracy is. It's like in the constitution of the United States, which says that all men are created equal, but women could not vote until 1920. It means the government says one thing but doesn't do what it says.

One thing that is a difference between what is said and what really is has to do with how people are treated at different ages. When you are 18, you can join the army and fight in a war and you can vote, but you can't buy a beer or glass of wine. And you can drive a car at age 16, but you can't live away from home and quit school. If a person is mature enough to drive, shouldn't they be able to make decisions about their life? If a person can fight in a war, shouldn't they be able to drink alcohol if they want? Just when is a person an adult? Some kids have babies when they are only 15 years old. Then they are supposed to act like an adult and take care of the baby, but if they don't have a baby, no one would ever give them a baby to take care of all by themselves. Sometimes things like this are just mixed up.

MYTHOLOGICAL MONSTERS

PAGE 49

Answers will vary. A sample answer:

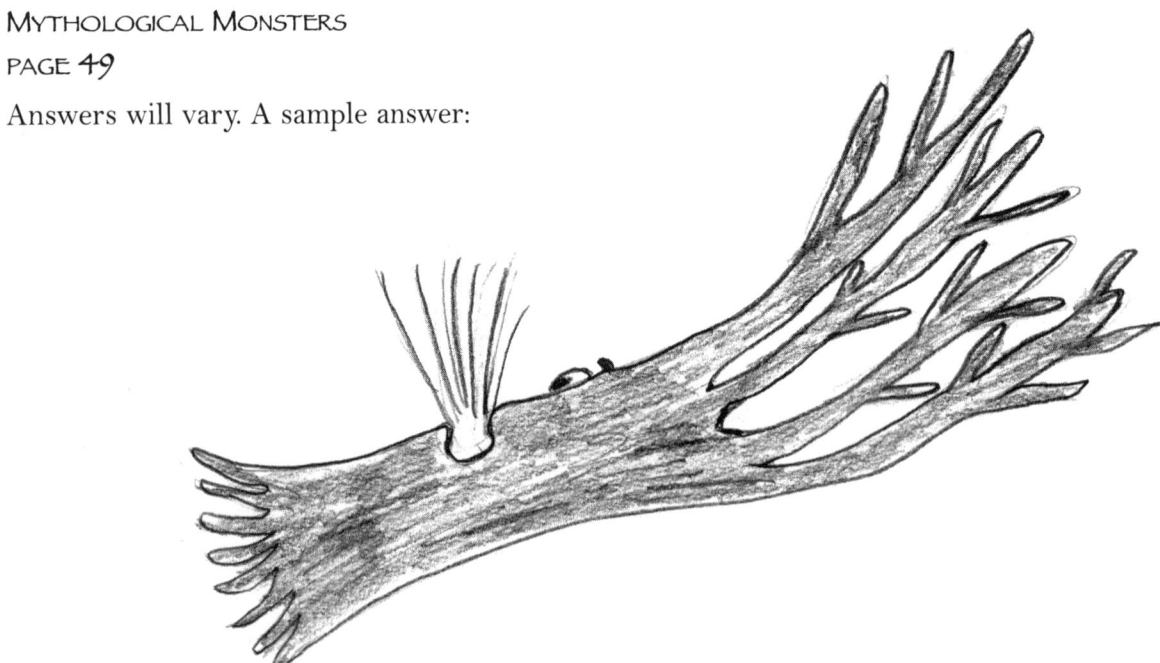

Oakley, the weather monster, is a giant black tree as big as a building with a face in the trunk that has a huge mouth. The roots are like many legs. Oakley has no leaves, but the branches are so big and powerful that they can move clouds around.

   Oakley can change the weather. If a family is driving to another state for the holidays, and they run into a snowstorm, they just call for Oakley on the cell phone and he will come and bring the sunshine. If an airplane is flying to California and it flies into hail and rain, then the pilot can radio a message to Oakley to blow away the storm. And if a kid gets a sled for Christmas and wants snow, she can call upon Oakley to bring snow, just on the sledding hill.

Oakley can read people's minds, so he knows if you are asking to change the weather for a good reason or a bad one. If you are trying to change the weather to hurt people, Oakley will cause worse weather for you. Oakley is very busy, especially in the winter and during tornado season in Iowa.

Extra Challenge

Once in a huge, dark forest in northern Maine, a giant tree grew bigger than all the rest. It was so tall that its branches brushed against the clouds. When the forest dried out because there was no rain, the tree poked the clouds until it started to rain. When snow blanketed the forest so heavily that all the branches were breaking off the trees, the giant tree pushed away the storm clouds with its branches.

One day, the giant tree noticed a bump on its root. When it poked at the bump, a new tree popped out and started to grow and grow and grow. Because it was so dark in the forest, the giant tree picked up the new tree and held it up in its highest branches to get a closer look. Just then, a mysterious powerful wind came along and blew the little tree away. The wind said to the tree, "I have just blown magic powers into you, even more powers than your father tree. From now on, you will be known as Oakley. Now go find what your powers may be."

The little tree then grew bigger and bigger as it flew over the land. It could feel a face forming in its trunk and when it started to fall from the sky, it blew with its mouth and rose higher in the sky. Oakley blew and blew and its mouth grew and grew. As Oakley kept blowing, he noticed that he could move the clouds. It was then that Oakley realized his magic powers — to move the clouds. And that's how the weather monster came to be.

Sue M.

A Poem of Epic Proportions
page 50

Answers will vary. A sample answer:

My Great Grandpa

Alex Trani was rather small—
Only 5'5", if even that tall.
But it didn't matter one little bit
'Cuz Alex Trani was tougher than spit.
Just off the boat from Italy,
He got a job at the rock quarry.
He mined limestone with a hack,
Then carried it up hill on his back.
He worked so hard, but always swore

America's better than Italy when you're poor.
His goal was to purchase a piece of land --
His own piece of America is what he planned.
His American dream he did fulfill
When he had his own land to cultivate and till.
He grew watermelon, eggplants, cucumbers and peas
And raised beautiful tomatoes to make spaghetti.
Alex Trani now had a good life,
So he decided to find himself a wife.
Fell in love and married the young Celestina,
who bore him Ann, Anthony, Silvio and Florino.
Sadly, his beautiful wife became deathly ill.
He could not save her, despite his strong will.
He raised his four children, alone everyday
Until he married the widow -- Ida Rae.
She brought to the marriage three kids of their own,
And with seven children, they had a lively home.
Alex Trani could be tough, mean and uncouth,
Still fiercely loved by his children and their children, too.
They all called him Papa and thought he was great,
But they'd never dare sass, question or disobey.
He was so hardy he punched a horse in the teeth
After that nasty horse kicked him square in his belly.
As you can see, Alex Trani knew no fear
'Cuz this incident happened in his seventieth year.
Old Papa Trani died in 1978
But had clearly overcome his predestined fate.
On the boat from Italy, as a teenaged lad
Alex sought to fulfill the vision he had.
By his death, he had achieved his aim —
A wonderful family and land in his name.

Dawn D.

THE SCHMIKINGS
WHAT'S THE REAL STORY?
PAGE 66

See teacher instructions, page 65.

RIDDLE ME THIS
PAGE 69

Examples are included in the exercise.

BALLADS

PAGE 70

Answers will vary. A sample answer:

THE BALLAD OF CYRANO DE BERGERAC
(Sing to the tune of "Oh, My Darling, Clementine")

Oh, poor darling!
Oh, poor darling!
Cyrano de Bergerac.
Though he was both brave and charming,
With Roxanne, he had no knack.

His biggest feature
Made him a creature
Of people's jokes, and made them stare.
They said his nose was so humongous
It could have been a dragon's lair.

Roxanne loved Christian.
He was so handsome.
So Cyrano helped out his friend
By writing poems Christian could give her,
So from him, they did pretend.

Christian felt guilty.
He thought that truly,
If she knew they weren't his lines,
That she'd love Cyrano so deeply
And would fall for him in time.

In the midst
Of his big guilt trip
Christian left to stop the strife
Of the war twixt France and Spain
And which cost Christian his life.

Oh, poor Roxanne,
Was such a big fan,
Of Christian's looks and poetry.
She heard the news and started sobbing.
Then retired to misery.

In a convent,
In a convent,
Roxanne spent all of her days
While Cyrano was slowly aging,
And had not a word to say.

One day Roxanne
Came to see him.
Cyrano had grown so old.
He was dying, she was crying,
But he felt he should be bold.

So he told her
It was he who
Wrote the poems Christian had read.
She was happy and she hugged him,
But he was on his deathbed.

Oh, my darlings!
Oh, my darlings!
Cyrano, Roxanne, apart.
Though a sad and awful ending,
He finally did win Roxanne's heart.

Sam P.

There's No Ages Like Dark Ages
What's the REAL Story?
page 87

See teacher instructions, pages 85-86.

Answer Keys

Design Your Own Coat of Arms
page 91

Answers will vary. A sample answer:

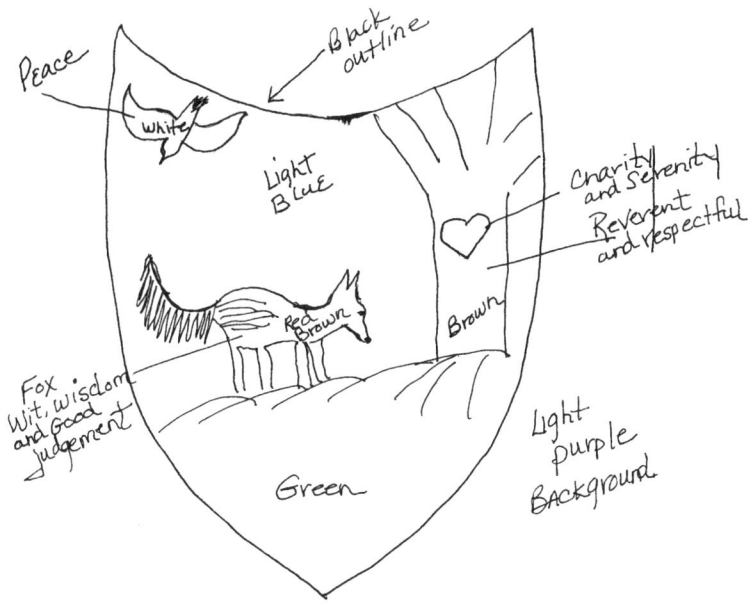

My Coat Of Arms represents the characteristics of my family. I think it reminds us of who we are and the things we should realize are important in what we do. Like a fox, we should use our wit, wisdom and good judgement in making decisions. Like a tree trunk, we should be reverent and respectful of other people in the world. The heart carved in the tree reminds us to be sincere in our thoughts and actions and also to be charitable toward those who have less. The dove of peace reminds us to be peaceful and to settle issues and disagreements in a non-violent way.

    The colors of the Coat of Arms are green, light blue and a light purple background behind the shield. The colors again remind us of family loyalty and love (green), to practice justice in the world (purple), and to be truthful in what we say and do (blue). The shield is outlined in black, which reminds us that everything on the shield is a constant part of our lives.

Mary G.

Alliteration
page 92

Answers will vary. A sample answer:

1. Through her binoculars, Bianca observed bunches of Backstreet Boys bumping into each other backstage.

2. Cuddly calico cats are capable of curling contentedly onto cotton coverlets for hours.

3. Fifty fabulous flamingoes fascinated us by fastidiously feeding on french fries and fish.

4. A moose who is outmaneuvered by a mouse is a miserable moose.

5. Pepperoni pizza with Pepsi is what pleases Pat's palate when she perches on the porch and ponders Plato.

Renaissance Reform School
What's the REAL Story?
page 107

See Teacher Instructions, pages 106

Renaissance People
page 108

Answers will vary. Sample answer:

MICHELANGELO BOYARDEE:
He painted the ceiling of garages and sheds.
He made sculptures of pyramids, using different materials.
He could cook.

MICHELANGELO BUONARROTI:
He is considered one of the greatest artists of all time.
He painted the ceiling of the Sistine Chapel.
He sculpted Biblical characters from marble.

LEONARDO DA LINGUINI:
He painted the "Moaning Lisa."
He played the spoons.
He could sing.
He juggled cantaloupes.
He was a clumsy juggler.
He could stand on his head for 43 minutes before passing out.
He could cook.

LEONARDO DA VINCI:
He painted the "Mona Lisa" and the "Last Supper."
He was a painter, sculptor, architect and engineer.
He had ideas ahead of his time about biology, aeronautics, hydrodynamics and other sciences.
He painted with Michelangelo.

DONNAJELLO:
He was an acrobat and tumbler.
He performed with his brother.
He fell a lot and broke things while performing.
He could cook.

DONATELLO:
He was a master of sculpture during the Renaissance.
He lived in Florence from 1386-1466.
He is known as the father of modern sculpture.

Handbook of Rules

page 109

Answers will vary. Sample answer:

Standard Modern Day Rules Handbook for During Detention
1. Don't drop your huge pile of books on the floor to wake up your friend who's asleep.
2. Don't fall asleep and drool on your desk.
3. Don't tap your pencil on your desk just to annoy the teacher.
4. Don't make faces at the teacher when you think he or she isn't looking.
5. Don't bring your pet hamster to keep you company.
6. Don't throw spit wads at the ceiling.
7. Don't try to sneak out of the room while the teacher is grading papers.
8. Don't make smart remarks and get another detention.
9. Don't pretend you're having a seizure so you can get out early.
10. Don't write on the desk.

About the Author

BRUCE BERGER has been a teacher for twenty years in Barrington, Illinois. Always interested in drama, he has acted, directed, and written plays in college and community theatre productions. He presently teaches sixth grade at Barrington Middle School-Station Campus, where he also spends a great deal of time coaching girls' and boys' basketball.

Berger lives in McHenry, Illinois, with his wife, Barb, and two children Tess and Adam.

Other Titles from Cottonwood Press

AbraVocabra
The amazingly sensible approach to teaching vocabulary..................................$21.95

Attitude!
Helping students WANT to succeed in school and then setting them up for success...........$19.95

BEYOND Roses Are Red, Violets Are Blue
A practical guide for helping student write free verse....................................$19.95

Commas
Teaching students to use commas correctly, without boring them to tears..................$14.95

Did You Really Fall into a Vat of Anchovies?
Games and activities for English and language arts.......................................$18.95

A to Z
Novel ideas for reading teachers...$16.95

Games for English and Language Arts
Reproducible games that challenge students..$18.95

Hide Your Ex-Lax Under the Wheaties
Poems about schools, teachers, kids and education..$7.95

Hot Fudge Monday
Tasty ways to teach parts of speech to students who have a hard time swallowing anything to do with grammar..$19.95

How to Flunk, How to Pass Poster Set
Two humorous posters that give great advice..$6.95

Ideas that Really Work!
Activities for English and language arts...$21.95

If They're Laughing . . .
Ideas for using humor effectively in the classroom, even if you're not funny yourself..........$12.95

Promise You Won't Get Mad
And other read-aloud plays for young adults..$15.95

Journal Jumpstarts
Quick topics and tips for journal writing..$7.95

A Month of Fundays
A whole year of games and activities for just about every holiday you've ever heard of, and many that you haven't..$23.95

Quotation Marks
Teaching the correct use of quotation marks through mini-lessons that won't put students to sleep...$12.95

Reluctant Disciplinarian
   Advice on classroom management from a softy who became (eventually) a successful teacher $14.95

Short and Sweet
   Quick creative writing activities that encourage imagination, humor and enthusiasm for writing $10.95

Survival Tips for New Teachers
   From people who have been there (and lived to tell about it) $7.95

Surviving Last Period on Fridays and Other Desperate Situations
   A game book for language arts..$14.95

ThoughtWorks
   Imaginative problem-solving activities for small groups $14.95

When They Think They Have Nothing to Write About . . .
   Over 125 practical composition activities based on the writing process $14.95

Writing Your Life
   Autobiographical writing activities for young people $14.95

AND MORE!

TO ORDER MORE COPIES OF TIME WARPED

Please send me _____ copies of *Time Warped*. I am enclosing $21.95, plus shipping and handling ($4.00 for one book, $2.00 for each additional book). Colorado residents add 66¢ sales tax per book. Total amount $_____.

Name _____

School _____
(Include only if using school address.)

Address _____

City _____ State _____ Zip Code _____

Method of Payment:

❏ Payment enclosed   ❏ Visa/MC/Discover   ❏ Purchase Order

Credit Card# _____ Expiration Date _____

Signature _____

Send to:

Cottonwood Press, Inc.
107 Cameron Drive
Fort Collins, CO 80525
1-800-864-4297
www.cottonwoodpress.com

Or call for a free catalog of practical materials for English and language arts, grades 5-12.

COTTONWOOD PRESS INC.